I0593890

FAIR DAY

FAIR DAY

Alex Dunkin

Buon-Cattivi Press

Adelaide, Australia

Published by the Buon-Cattivi Press, 2017
Adelaide, Australia

ISBN (PAPERBACK) 978-0-9953661-4-5
ISBN (EBOOK) 978-0-9953661-5-2

Book design and cover art by Andrew Crooks
Printed by IngramSpark

Thanks to Enza, Ioana and Greg for years of encouragement and mentoring to help me complete this novel.

To the many friends and family who supported me on the trek to research, write and polish *Fair Day* within a tight deadline.

Fair Day was supported through an Australian Government Research Training Program Scholarship.

Pre-ramble: The delightful moment of half time when the men can truly come together

The stench of sweat and piss greet the men back into the change rooms. The roars from the crowd echo down the corridor but are cut off by the door snapping shut.

'Oh thank Christ,' Buck says as he sits in front of his mirror. 'I'm so glad it's half time. I don't think I could've lasted another five minutes without a solid break,' he adds, touching the tips of his hair.

'Solid effort blokes,' their captain Swanny shouts, 'but we can't stop now just because we're ahead. Get prepped. We need another half like that one, always on the mark and straight for the goal. No short games. That's what the Westies do best and we can't play it their way.'

Ryan sits down next to Buck with a huff. He flicks the switch to his mirror lights.

'What's up, bae?' Buck asks.

'Nothin',' Ryan sighs. 'He's just such a bitch.'

'Who?'

'You know. Hayden. Last year we were best mates playing for the same team, and now he's playing for those Westie slags, standing there snarkin' behind my back. What a dead-set two-faced moll,' Ryan curses. He pushes his face towards his mirror and stretches his skin with expert fingers. 'Can you believe these pores?'

Buck places his jar of wax back down next to his hair straightener and turns to face Ryan.

'Ah, that's nothing,' he dismisses. 'Look at these suckers.' Buck pinches the skin around his eyes to emphasise the crow's feet. 'At least you're still young and don't have to worry about wrinkles. Look how smooth your skin is.'

'I know. I'm just really feeling down. I just don't understand what I've done for Hayden to be so mean. I even invited him to my birthday party. He said he'd come but flaked on me. Then on Facebook I saw he spent the entire day with one of his new teammates. What's he got that I don't have?'

Swanny centres himself in the room. He wipes a speck of lint from his guernsey and plucks a stray hair from his arm.

'Right-o bitches,' he shouts. 'Fall in, let's get revved up.'

Buck turns to Ryan and places a comforting hand on his shoulder.

'Don't worry about Hayden,' he soothes. 'You're not on the same team anymore. He's obviously moved on. You should too. Ignore what he says. And besides, you have us. We're all still here for you.'

'Thanks,' Ryan says, the emotion of the moment glistening in his eyes. 'You've always been a bestie to me.'

Ryan stands up from the mirror as a pumped jeer bellows around the room. The locker room doors open with the accompaniment of the crowd's roar. The men smack each other on the arse as they disgorge themselves onto the sporting field to seek another victory.

PART I

From this time forward, under God, I pledge my loyalty to Australia and its people, whose democratic beliefs I share, whose rights and liberties I respect, and whose laws I will uphold and obey.

Cassandra

'Good morning. This is Cassandra Cummings with your 5CCB morning news update. Founders Bay is heating up again for Australia Day. It is the tenth consecutive day over thirty-five degrees and the current heatwave is forecast to continue for five more days. The region's fire alert level remains at extreme and a total fire ban is in place across the state.

'In politics, the Prime Minister has announced new investment incentives for the mining industry in an attempt to increase Australian jobs in electricity production, stating that "the coal industry holds a prominent position within Australia's past and present-day landscape" and that "without coal world energy production would not be as it is today".

'Looking at local news, a record number of tourists and

beachgoers are expected in Founders Bay for the Australia Day holiday. Authorities remind people to drink responsibly and take care out on the beaches and in the sun. The far northern waters off Founders Bay have been declared a no go zone due to a sudden influx of bluebottle jellyfish.

'In sports, local hero Dwayne Story has qualified for the Beer Pong World Championships. The local footy star kicked one hundred goals for his tenth season in a row and says that the change of code is a challenging and rewarding experience for him.

'Sunny and forty-one today. I'm Cassandra Cummings. Join me again in an hour for the next 5CCB news update.'

Claire and David

'It's so fuckin' hot,' David mutters. 'Why do we have to do this every year?'

'It wouldn't be a problem if you just sucked it up and had the aircon fixed,' Claire snaps back. She knows driving in this weather isn't ideal. A juicy layer of sweat lines her singlet as they cruise along the highway with their windows up. 'Besides, it's the best place for the Australia Day holiday. Uncle Simon always has the best location, best booze and Tony has the best contact for your weed.'

David grunts and leans forward to encourage the stale air to evaporate some of the stickiness off his back.

'Just open the window,' Claire says.

'Can't. They're broken too.'

'What the hell? Just buy a new car. You're not an apprentice anymore, you can afford something that at least works.'

'Yeah but me and Sheila go way back,' David beams. His hand reaches out and affectionately strokes the steering wheel. Claire rolls her eyes and glances out the window at the rolling bushland.

'We must be getting close,' she says, observing the ancient gums thinning out to shorter shrubs that are little more than a thick mass of brown twigs. A slow-building scent of salt seeps into the car, sparking memories deep within Claire. She remembers all the years she has come to see her uncle at his house nestled in Founders Bay, a charming town of two thousand that swells with vacationers at the merest whiff of a public holiday. She's looking forward to the glide of sweet wines across her tongue at any hour and from any bottle she likes while her uncle hosts, and the late night skinny dips to cool her skin against the sweltering heat that relentlessly blasts the town during summer.

'Why can't we visit your parents one year?' David asks.

'Because they live down south and it's too friggin' cold. And you didn't seem to be so upset last time you came here. We'll be fine once we get there.'

'I know. It's just... your uncles. They're so...'

'So what?'

'They're so gay,' David says.

Grant

'Now boy, you stay in here for the day,' Grant says glancing down at his beloved pet. 'We don't want a repeat of last year now do we? You have plenty of food and water for the day. It's cool enough in here as well, so you don't need to make a sound.'

Grant shuts the cellar door as he leaves, casting the room behind it into darkness. He inhales and shivers excitedly. The aroma of baking bread spreads throughout the entire house. No doubt the scent has spread to the top floor and woken the dormant teenagers. Grant sighs, knowing Facebook and Twitter would have kept them up all night but the smell of their mother's bread on Australia Day always sparks a fresh child-like obedience. The guests would be arriving soon, Grant would need to get cracking on the barbeque to be in time for lunch, and get cracking on the booze to have any hope of making it through the day with his sanity intact. He reconsiders the single six-pack in his hand, then sharply turns and heads back into the cellar.

A soft whimper sounds in the back corner as the door

seals the cool air in the cellar.

'It's okay boy, I'm just grabbing myself some more beer,' Grant croons to soothe his boy's nerves. 'I don't think she'll be down today. She's got too much to do upstairs,' he adds in a whisper. The pet retreats to the comfort of his bed, his calm breaths escape into the darkness.

Simon

'Hello darling,' Simon trills, arms wide ready for an embrace, then draws back as he notices the moisture running off Claire's body. 'I would hug you but you look like you've run a marathon.'

'Hey Uncle Simon,' Claire doesn't attempt to hug her uncle. 'You remember my boyfriend, David.'

'Of course I remember the lovely David. Good to see we didn't scare you off last year. Tony's around here somewhere, no doubt sweeping out the sand again. He should know by now he'll never get it all,' Simon says, embracing David, sweat-drenched shirt and all. David flinches. 'You definitely need a shower. You know where everything is Claire. We've left the usual room free for you. Lunch shouldn't be for a while so take your time.' Simon winks. It is difficult to tell if it's due to a scent in the air or simply a unique ability to know when people were going to have sex. He recalls Claire's complaint in her emails that living with four housemates made it difficult for her to have her boyfriend over for more than a silent quickie.

Claire and David

Claire steps into the shower to find countless grains of sand already there, as always. The grains scratch against her feet, triggering memories of vintage port and sand in her expensive bra the morning after Australia Day last year. Naked skin flashes through her mind. The exposure of the memory tingles through her.

'Well, come here often?' David drawls in his sexiest tone.

'Hello there sailor,' Claire flirts. David stands naked, the curtain pulled aside to show the hairlessness of his body. 'It's for the sports tape,' he would say, yet Claire knows he likes the feel of his own bare skin. 'I suppose I do come here often enough,' Claire answers, even though she knows that being their first encounter for a while it will last five minutes at most. 'And it was only going to be a quick visit today, but it looks like something has come up,' she purrs, reaching down for his erection.

IT'S THAT TIME OF YEAR, BACK TO SCHOOL TIME.
ARE YOU READY? ALL YOUR BACK TO SCHOOL

Ronald

'Good morning Australia, this is Ronald Ray with your Today's Affairs news brief. Tonight, Michelle Kim presents her exclusive interview with a local government official who reveals the true cost of alternative Australia Day events.'

'Thanks Ronald. This is Michelle Kim for Today's Affairs. I'm here with a local government source, who has requested anonymity for fear that she will be prosecuted for revealing this exclusive story. For the purposes of this interview we will call her Sharon.

'Why have you come to us with this information?'

'This has gone on for too long. It's become outrageous.'

'And what is it that has become outrageous?'

'These Survival Day events. They go too far and have

become too expensive.'

'Are you aware of the risks posed to yourself by enlightening the Australian public with this news?'

'I do. But I knew as a fair dinkum Australian it is my duty to make sure people know how much money is being spent on Survival Day just so *they* can have their own events on Australia Day. Australia Day is about inclusion and everyone doing the same thing to celebrate the creation of our nation with the first fleet. If they don't like it they should leave.'

'Incredible. This is Michelle Kim for Today's Affairs. Back to you Ronald.'

'Outrageous. Thanks Michelle. Tune in at seven-thirty tonight for the full interview plus more. I'm Ronald Ray. I will be back after Doctor Doctor with your next Today's Affairs new brief.'

Simon

Simon returns to the kitchen as soon as Claire has left for the shower. She knows the ropes and he has plenty of his own business to take care of before lunch is ready. The chilli sizzling over the stove singes his nose hairs. He hopes fervently as always that the egregious chilli and the liberal application of booze will disguise his poor cooking. He throws the meat into the mix and stirs with one hand, reaching for the opened bottle of red with the other. Simon loosely grips the bottle neck and expertly tips the contents into his waiting glass, not once looking away from the mince frying in the heat.

'Yes please,' Tony sings as he enters the kitchen, empty wine glass in hand. 'Did I just hear Claire come in?'

'You did,' Simon answers while pouring his partner some red. 'She's still with that fresh piece.'

'Oh nice. No doubt he'll be asking me for a little something later on,' Tony pushes his fingers to his mouth suggestively. 'Maybe I could get a little something in return.'

'Oh the cheek,' Simon retorts playfully, knowing it's all light-hearted for now. Even with all their Australia Day traditions, the mischief that Tony is able to get himself into is beyond Simon's ability to plan.

Timmo

'Chuck us a tinnie will ya?' Timmo yells over the bass. Jonno reaches into the Esky under his feet in the front seat and throws a can of beer back to Timmo. 'Cheers mate.'

'D'ya reckon we'll be early enough to score a good spot on the beach?' Jacko shouts from the driver's seat. The remnants of a durrie glow between his fingertips.

'Yeah, no wuckers,' Timmo calls back. 'If it's the same as last year everyone'll be at the memorials and ceremony things with the mayor until lunch.'

'Fuckin' muzzos,' Jacko spits. 'More of 'em get government backing to take all our jobs.' He flicks the butt out the window and onto the highway. Jacko's beast leads the four-car entourage, which speeds past the fading ember straight toward Founders Bay's famous beach for their barbecue of the year.

HAVE YOU GOT YOUR VERY OWN MINIBAKERMIX PRO™? IT'S THE ALL-IN-ONE GADGET THAT EVERYONE IS TALKING ABOUT. IT BAKES. IT MIXES. IT EVEN CLEANS ITSELF AT THE TOUCH OF A BUTTON. THE MINIBAKERMIX PRO™ HAS TAKEN AMERICA BY STORM. NINE OUT OF TEN PEOPLE SURVEYED SAID THEY DON'T HAVE TO USE ANY OTHER KITCHEN APPLIANCES SINCE THEY BOUGHT THEIR VERY OWN MINIBAKERMIX PRO™. IT'S SUCH AN EASY PRODUCT TO USE. JUST ADD THE INGREDIENTS AND SELECT ONE OF THE PRE-PROGRAMMED SETTINGS AND THE MINIBAKERMIX PRO™ DOES THE REST FOR YOU. BUT THAT'S NOT ALL. CALL 1800-MBM-PRO NOW AND YOU'LL RECEIVE A FREE KNIFE SET AND SANDWICH PRESS. THAT'S NOT ONE, NOT TWO, BUT THREE AMAZING PRODUCTS ALL FOR THE ONE LOW PRICE. DON'T MISS OUT ON THIS

Grant

The gas flame ignites quickly underneath Grant's Weber. The smell of old burning fat lifts instantly off the grills. Grant cringes at the extra heat scorching his face.

'Starting a bit early, aren't we?' Helen asks from the veranda. She wheels around the outside glass table, placing napkins and cutlery meticulously into position.

'Nah. I want to give the chicken plenty of time to roast. I don't want to be responsible for poisoning anyone. The rest of the meat can wait until everyone else gets here.' He looks up to his wife. She is still as stunningly perfect as the day they met. A white breezy summer dress hangs loosely from the string around her neck. Grant admires how everything on the front is held together with a lace-inspired apron that will be ripped off at the last moment before their guests arrive to reveal the perfectly bright dress underneath. 'Shouldn't it be ten adults this year?' he says, counting the seats.

'No silly,' Helen sighs. 'Jane and Danielle aren't quite old enough yet. Once they're able to drink then I'll add extra seats for them.'

'They might not be old enough to drink but Jane sure knows how to,' Grant smirks, recalling Jane's Facebook photos from her joint birthday with Danielle, courtesy of her complete disinterest in self-censorship. *For a seventeen-year-old she has a lot of photos featuring vomit*, Grant chuckles to himself. Helen surveys the prepared tables. Her head bobs along as she silently counts the items spread before her. An uncertain grin eases onto her face while she circles the table for a final time. She gently reaches out and adjusts by a few centimetres the position of a jug of water with sliced lemon. Content, she brushes her hands on her apron and quietly retreats behind the glass doors to the kitchen.

Grant fiddles the marinated chicken into the barbecue, drops the lid and steps back to the relative coolness of the sunlight. *Same as last year*, he thinks to himself, *bloody hot*. He consoles himself with the shimmering blue water of the stretch of ocean overlooked by their veranda. Memories float up of its coolness last year and how the water's stillness allowed them to float for hours without being dragged out to sea. This year however the heavy undertow is made obvious by the long drag marks after every wave. A string of marquees form a dotted trail of shade along the beach. He looks back to his house. Helen is easy to spot through the floor-to-ceiling windows. She'd spent hours polishing those windows when they first arrived. Every few moments she glances out the kitchen window onto the irradiated beach before fussing again amongst the salads and pastries. Grant sighs in appreciation of the two-storey structure that stands solidly before him. Glistening sunlight beams off the many windows. At the right time of the evening he will open the doors on the balcony and the sweet summery breeze will fill the house.

Grant looks over to his neighbours. The structure on his left is a fitting companion to his own, drawing a nod of satisfaction, but he then cringes as his vision sweeps over the house to the right. The place where asbestos came to die. Grant shakes his head. This oasis had been prime real estate almost from the moment the surrounding dunes were declared a nature strip, giving the three residential properties already there an exclusive privacy. Two of the properties have been developed into the palaces their positions demanded, and Grant had worked hard to make his contribution to that. The third is a tumbledown shack on the edge of collapse, its sandy veranda a stark contrast to his vast sprawl of immaculate Tuscan pavers. The surrounding scrub encroached right up to his neighbour's door like a welcome mat, mocking his own manicured garden.

As he watches, the back door slides open on his neighbour's house. A man in scant Speedos darts out to the shower attached to the veranda pole, tosses a towel over a nearby deck chair and turns on the water.

'Oh, hello Grant,' Tony waves across the fence. He points over his back to the running water. 'The other one's taken. They might be a while,' he winks.

Grant shakes his head with a smile and waves back. *Fuckin' perverts*, he thinks.

Mayor Keith MacDonald cringes at the sight of his mayoral robe and livery collar. Rubbing his shoulder he sighs in anticipation of the weight that will tax him as much as his duties do. It would be the same as every year: he'd have to don the red gowns and stand in the heat for the Survival Day memorial, then he'd have to rush off to don the thicker black robes and stand in the heat for a bunch of new citizens to recite their pledge to the country at the naturalisation ceremony and then he'd have to dash off to don the blue robes to officiate the Australia Day awards celebration.

'Bunch of hard workers, the lot of them,' Keith says. He struggles to perfect the tie around his neck.

'The what now, luv?' Dot asks.

'The immigrants, dear. The ones around this town are always working or volunteering with the CFS. I don't see what the fuss is about.'

'Fear for their own jobs, luv. Same as always. Australians first and all.'

'What a load of nonsense,' Keith leads into his usual spiel. 'Any Australian out here can have a job in this town in a heartbeat if they wanted it. I kid you not, just yesterday I had Darryl from the meatworks complaining that he's struggling to fill fifty positions. Like they do every month. They've pushed to have so many migrants settle here because no one else will take the job. That's the reason I have to suffer through these bloody ceremonies and welcomes so often, just so they have enough workers to scrape shit and guts off an abattoir floor.'

'Well, after today there'll be a few more Australians to fill those positions, darl,' Dot suggests. She plucks fluff from the mayoral robes. She turns her attention to the tie around her husband's neck. Three tosses of the silk later and a tidy knot tightens around Keith's throat. 'Wait a second. Are you going to be saying goodbye to Ralph before you get into your formal robes?'

'Well of course I would do that,' Keith replies.

'Go do that now before I help you with the rest of the robes. God knows they take forever to wash.'

'No worries dear,' Keith says. 'I'll do that now.'

Keith strolls in his half-done suit down the short, carpeted corridor to the back door. Ralph and his dirty red coat shake erratically with excitement. The shivers and quivers dislodge a fresh batch of fur onto the ground.

'Hello gorgeous,' Keith gushes. 'Are you gonna miss me? Don't worry. I won't be gone all day. Just until dinner.' The kelpie returns the affection with vigorous licks of the mayor's black shoes. Saliva polishes the leather on Keith's feet. Keith laughs deeply.

'I'll never understand,' Dot pipes in from the fly-screen door. 'So much love I will never know.'

'The bond between a man and his beast will never be fully understood, hun.' He turns to the licking tongue of

Ralph. 'We'll be home soon, yes we will, we'll be home soon,' he coos in his most sickly baby voice.

'He's a work dog. You shouldn't spoil him.'

'Yes, but the sweetie has worked hard for me, and I just can't help it with my little poppet.'

'You've been saying that since he was a pup,' Dot whispers to herself.

'Goodbye boy. See you at dinner,' Keith wraps up. 'We'll have more workers in this town before the sun goes down.'

Timmo

'FAAARRK!' Jacko shouts from the edge of the sand. In his enthusiasm he had bounced barefoot from the driver's seat straight onto the beach, leaving everyone else to unload. 'The sand is burning already. Same as last year.'

'Chuck ya thongs on,' Timmo shouts without raising his head from the car boot.

The four Holdens and a lone duck Falcon monopolise half the car park nestled between the exclusive, poshed-up shacks and the rest of the town. Timmo reckons the rolling white sand is the best on this side of the country. Despite its beauty the three hundred kay trip means only a few thousand people rock up to share the big-arse stretch of beach. Even with an extra few thousand people there'd be loads of space to chuck a cat or six around before you hit the person next to you. It's huge, leaving tons of space for Timmo and his mates to set up camp.

'We gunna set up in the same place?' Timmo asks while negotiating the stumps and wickets into his arms. 'Is the flat patch still there?'

'Yeah, looks like it,' Jacko shouts back, cooling his feet at the standalone public shower. 'I don't know why I bother. This water is just as fucking hot. Hey Tamie babe, can you bring me my towel?'

'Get it yerself, prick,' Tamie calls from the boot of her car. She heaves a huge marquee bag out of the boot while her mates Caitlin and Karen charge away from her car to the water with their towels. 'I'm not your babe anymore. You can get it yerself. Dickhead.' *Three years wasted on sex and booze*, she thinks to herself. *At least the booze was mostly good.* Tamie flicks her sandy blond plait over her shoulder and tucks it under her shirt. She whips off the light fabric over her head to reveal a patriotic bikini and matching boardies. The Union Jack sits proudly on her right boob and the Southern Cross on her left. She lifts out an Esky full of Cruisers and makes her way down to the beach, marquee dragging behind her. The rest of the supplies can eventually go up to Timmo's dad's pad to keep it all within stumbling distance of clean dunnies.

'Fine,' Jacko mutters. He stomps past Tamie straight back to his own car. His thongs lie waiting under his seat. The cheap rubber hits the ground with a slap. 'Gunna be an awkward Straya Day,' he adds as he grabs his towel and turns to walk back to the beach.

'Why's that?' Jonno asks, juggling his own Esky and several Cottonvalue bags full of junk food.

'Why do you think?'

'I reckon it's cos she dumped you two weeks back and spent those two weeks hooking up with most of the blokes we came here with to get back at you.'

'Sounds about right. Can't fucking believe you fucking went there. You know the rules. Bros first dude.'

'Yeah, but come on. It's Tamie, she's hot. We were both shitfaced anyway.'

'Doesn't make it any better.'

'Did for me. Now give us a hand will ya and grab an Esky and deck chair. Let's crack a few Bundies and remember this is just the beginning of a fresh year.'

Jacko sighs. 'Fine. I reckon I need a few shots before we head down to join everyone else.'

WANT THE BEST FOR MAN'S BEST FRIEND? NEW
DENTAL DOG BITES ARE AVAILABLE NOW. THE
IMPROVED DENTAL DOG FORMULA HAS EXTRA
CHEWY BITS TO HELP KEEP YOUR LOVED ONE'S
TEETH CLEAN. DENTAL DOG COMES IN A VARIETY

OF REAL MEAT FLAVOURS THAT YOUR DOG WON'T
BE ABLE TO RESIST.

Simon

'Feeling better, Claire?' Simon asks from the kitchen with a wink.

'Much better,' Claire plays up to his suspicions. She knows David makes a little too much noise for the shower to dampen. 'Where's Tony?' she asks, adjusting her fresh bikini and sarong.

'Probably outside harassing the neighbours.'

'Oh, Grant and Helen? They still live there? I really like them. They seemed to loosen up after a few drinks last time.'

'Yeah, they're not too bad, but there's something about them. I haven't really spoken to them since last year. I can't pin it down completely. I wonder if it's just that they're a bit homophobic but Tony's never got that impression. I always see them scowling when they look in this direction.'

'I think they just don't like your house,' Claire laughs. 'Just look at your neighbours' houses. The three properties along this strip are massively exclusive. Your two neighbours have mansions and you have a tumbledown shack.'

Simon glares at Claire.

'Here, cut some onion rings,' he asks. 'I always get emotional when I do it. And besides, we actually live here full-time, they just use their houses—no, I mean mansions—as shacks. Every year the house at the end is just full of bogan pissheads hijacking daddy's lovenest while he's overseas. And the house isn't that bad, at least now that I've hidden the bits that have fallen off in the ceiling.'

'Just an insurance case waiting to happen,' Claire smirks.

'Well, there's that,' Simon answers. 'Plus Tony doesn't like big changes.'

'Why don't you just buy him something shiny?' she asks with a quick glance around the room. Simon doesn't answer. He turns quickly and puts his hands to mixing a green salad. 'What? No response to that one?' Claire continues to joke. 'You know I'm right. Something pretty is all you'd need to distract him while you build a palace.'

A man clears his throat behind Claire. She doesn't need to turn around, she can already feel the figurative burn of his infamous glare. There's no other option, so she turns to face it. The widened whites of Tony's eyes exaggerate the sheer intensity of his blue glare. His face remains eerily still. Even the wrinkles disappear from his face as if burnt away by his outrage. A single droplet of water dares to drip from his hair and down his cheek, and miraculously it doesn't boil away. Claire follows it with her eyes. It visibly shrinks in size as it slides straight toward the concrete floor.

'Oh Tony, you know what I mean,' Claire tries. Tony just stares. 'It's just a joke.'

Tony finally blinks and his face relaxes a little. The

shimmery tension in the room eases cautiously along with Claire's heart rate. It's a rare experience to witness Tony's glare, let alone survive one.

'You'll have to visit us once over Easter. Less booze, more card games. You guys might be sober enough to remember more of what I tell you about the history of this house.' Tony lifts the towel to his hair as he talks and walks off, drying himself.

'You got off lightly,' Simon returns to the conversation. 'When I suggested an open relationship he kept that stare going for weeks.'

'Ick! TMI, Uncle Simon,' Claire eagerly turns her attention to the onions, her nerves and heart racing.

Mark

Mark's hand slaps across his bedside table in search of the obnoxious tweeting noise. He smacks the glass on the table, spilling the mouthful of remaining water across the floor and onto his socks.

'Argh. *Tranquillity* my arse,' he groans.

His fingers grasp onto his vibrating iPhone and slide across the screen to switch off his alarm. It was a late night home from work yesterday. *Think about the double time,* Mark reminds himself at the thought of returning to work on a public holiday. *It's for the money.*

Flopping weakly, Mark's arms and legs drag him out of the bed and towards the bathroom. Deep inside the house he can hear the muffled sounds of the shower and Triple J already cranking. His housemate is up and getting himself ready for work as well. *One day's work today between us and we'll be sweet for two weeks*, Mark tells himself.

Mark walks past the bathroom and straight into the kitchen. A tin of Nescafé awaits him next to the kettle. The sustenance of the instant mud will fuel him until he can grab a proper coffee from the café next to work. Until then he fumbles for one of the surviving mugs, loads sugar in with the instant coffee and water and walks back to his room.

Mark shuts the door with a creak and grimaces at the sight of his uniform on the ground. He places the coffee down and grabs the shirt. A few rough shakes, a whiff of the armpit and the shirt has passed his quality control regimen. He slides into the stiff synthetic fabric, finds his pants and shoes, and readies to leave the house.

'Adam could be hours in the bathroom,' he mutters to himself. 'Especially if his current shag is over.'

Buried under a moldering sock and a plate from last night's dinner he finds his car keys. Outside he makes the five step dash under the glaring sun and dives into the shade of his VT. Mark shudders at the thought of walking to work in the heat and looks at his metal cage of a car. *It's only a two minute drive*, he shrugs as he throws himself into the already sticky car.

Grant

The doorbell chimes at the front door. Helen effortlessly whips off her apron and tucks it into a drawer near the sink. A quick glide past the mirror, a miniscule corrective flick of her hair and she's ready to greet the arrivals. The wooden door heaves open allowing a blast of hot air to fire into the house.

'That air conditioner feels wonderful Helen,' her sister Margaret says as she leans in to peck Helen's cheeks. 'Grant,' she repeats the two peck ritual.

'Hello Arthur,' Grant holds out his hand and grips onto Arthur's with as much firm strength as he can muster. 'I'm guessing you would love a beer after that drive.'

'Absolutely,' Arthur responds. 'But none of that Victorian crap you sometimes have. A proper Aussie beer is in order.'

'Nothing wrong with a VB every now and then.'

'Sure, as long as you've numbed your tastebuds on shiraz or whiskey first.'

'Boys,' Helen says. 'Take it outside. You can fire up the barbecue now. It doesn't matter if the meat comes out early. I'm sure the kids are starving by now, they didn't come down for breakfast. Hello Jane, my how you've blossomed,' Helen adds to her niece.

Jane barely glances up from her iPhone.

'Hey,' she huffs and returns to tapping on the screen.

'You're dressed, um, lovely,' Helen says, running a critical eye over the fluorescent pink bikini and matching boardies with the tanned flesh almost outshining the thin straps. Jane grunts.

'Use your manners, young lady,' Margaret commands.

'God, fine. Thank you Aunty Helen, you're looking lovely as well. You too Uncle Grant, very butch.'

'Jane! Right that's it. Any more remarks like that and I'll cut you off from your phone for the day. You'll have to communicate with everyone in the traditional way.'

'Whatever,' Jane rolls her eyes. 'Is Dani here?'

'Yes, she's up in her room. You know the way,' Helen says.

Jane pushes past the adults and clicks her thongs up the stairs to the bedrooms.

'I'm so sorry about that,' Margaret says, her voice chasing Jane up the stairs.

'Don't worry about it,' Grant replies. 'I'm sure we'll be dealing with that sort of behaviour from Danielle at some point. So far she's been pretty good, although it's rare to see her off Facebook or whatever it is they're into these days.'

'As long as it's not Tinder,' Arthur mutters.

'What's that?'

'I get the impression it's social media for overloaded hormones. Keep an eye out for it,' Margaret cautions. 'Do you need any help setting up Helen?'

'Yes please. I'm just about to make up the punch for the kids.' Helen takes off towards the kitchen with Margaret in tow. Grant and Arthur follow, ducking to the fridge for beer and meat on their way to the barbecue area.

'Gosh, this heat,' Arthur moans as soon as the backdoor shuts leaving him and Grant alone outside.

'I know what you mean. Helen still wants to have a barbecue lunch out on the veranda and you know my wife gets what she wants.'

'Don't we all know you give her that,' Arthur teases and lifts his stubby to his lips.

'Manners don't last with you, do they?'

'My manners are immaculate, especially when our wives are around. How strict are those sisters?'

'You have no idea.'

Helen

'How is everything going with the family?' Margaret asks as she slices into a lemon.

'Everything is going well. It looks like Nicholas will make the honour roll again this year. Danielle's still the more creative one, she's thinking about curating an art exhibition for her individual project next year,' Helen says.

'That's great. And with Grant? Have things improved since Christmas?'

'Whatever do you mean? Oh, of course everything is fine.'

'Everything?' Margaret allows a smirk to sneak onto her lips.

'Well I think we're coming out of that stage now and progressing a bit. It was nice but I think I just like to be completely in control when we have special time together without having to worry about anything else getting in the way.'

'Mum! Gross!' Nicholas shouts from the base of the stairs. Margaret giggles to herself and moves the punch jug over to the sink ready for ice.

'Sorry Nicholas. We need to put a bell on you,' Helen blushes. 'Where's your rash vest?' she adds as she notices he's wearing only Billabong boardies.

IN HIS TIME AS A UNION LEADER ROBERT BUTCHER SUPPORTED THE CORRUPT ACTIONS OF NOW JAILED CONVICT JOHN RICHARDS. NOW HE WANTS TO BE PRIME MINISTER. HE'S BACKED CRIMINALS BEFORE. WHAT IS HE HIDING NOW? AUTHORISED BY DAISY ROSE OF THE CHRISTIAN LIBERALIST PARTY, MELBOURNE.

Helen

'Mum, I'm fourteen. I don't need a shirt when I'm swimming anymore.'

'Ok, just make sure you have lots of sunscreen on. It's a stinker out there.'

'SPF50+, mum.'

'Very good. Remember to reapply every hour.'

'Mum, SPF-*fifty*. I should be fine for the day.'

'Not if you sweat or go in the water,' Helen cautions at her son's back as he leaves the house. The door slams shut behind him.

'Whoops,' Margaret says, turning to face Helen again. 'Have you given him the talk yet?'

'No, that's Grant's job, though I have my doubts about his ability to do it without giggling like you just did,' Helen says.

Margaret lowers her eyes away from her sister's gaze and focuses on adding the ginger ale to the punch. She grabs a few slices of lime and lemon and drops them in at the same time.

'Is that mum's punch recipe?' Helen asks. 'She always made the best things. I was just going to go with my own.'

'It is mum's old recipe but I've added my own special twist.'

'I love her recipes. You must lend me her recipe book next time we catch up.'

The doorbell rings again, echoing down the tiled corridor.

'That must be Aunty Liz and her family.'

'They all came?'

'No, just her, Uncle Philip, Zac and Rodney.'

'Phew, I'm glad they're both independent bachelors again. I couldn't stand Rodney's children,' Margaret says as she drops the mint into the punch.

got fucken band from wearing an aussie flag at rev it up fest #unaustralian #aussiepride

Jonno Carlton, Jacko McCarthy and 56 others like this

Timmo

'Oi Jonno, chuck us another Bundy, wouldya,' Timmo calls from where he's sitting on his towel. A sudden smack of ice and aluminium crashes into his ribs. 'You prick!' Timmo cracks the can and wraps his lips around the opening to suck in the froth spewing forth.

'You gunna play cricket before it gets too hot?' Jonno asks. He stands over the wickets and hammers the wood into the sand with the bat.

'Inna minute. I'm gunna down this one and then open the house up so people can move their stuff in there.'

'Don't worry about that. We got all day to get into the house. This ball isn't going to bowl itself.'

'Just gimme a sec, mate,' Timmo throws back at him.

Tamie emerges from the ocean, kicking water as she stomps her way to the beach. Timmo pushes his sunnies down his nose as he watches her drag her feet up the sand and squeeze water from her whip of hair. The droplets roll over her tits and down the hump of her hips. She throws her hair back over her shoulder and strolls up to her Esky and towel. She reaches into the blue cooler and pulls out a coconut Cruiser.

'Hey Timmo,' she says, spotting his stare. She snatches up her towel and throws it down next to his. 'Thanks for having us over again. Well, thanks to your dad for letting us take over his place again.'

'Err, um... no probs Tam,' Timmo stutters back.

'Gosh, relax. Me and Jacko are through. You and me can chat and flirt as much as we want.'

'Well, um—I—I suppose we could.'

Tamie laughs and playfully slaps Timmo on his arm. Timmo feels Jacko's glare tingle on the back of his neck.

'Shit, I'm starting to roast already,' Tamie says. 'You got any sunscreen? I'm gunna be a bright ol' beetroot by the end of today. Last year I peeled for two weeks straight. That's why I bought that thing,' she nods her head to the unassembled marquee. 'Should be good once it gets real hot, that's if I can be arsed putting it up.'

'Yeah I got some Banana Boat.' Timmo turns back to the makeshift cricket pitch. 'Oi Jonno! Chuck us the sunscreen that's in with the Bundy.'

'Get it ya farken' self, slacker.'

'Carn mate. I asked nicely.'

Jonno reaches into the Esky to pluck out the sunscreen and lines up for the throw. He belts it across to Timmo, smacking him on the chest with a whack.

'Fuckin' cunt mate,' Timmo yelps. He turns back to Tamie. 'Here you go.'

'Cheers. Oh my god it's so cold. How long has it been in the Esky?' Tamie says, squirting a white blob into the palm of her hand.

'Since we left the city. I threw it in with the drinks to make sure I remembered it.'

'Could you do my back, Timmo?' she asks, pulling her hair over her shoulder to leave her pink flesh exposed.

'Um,' Timmo looks around quickly. 'Sure,' he responds hoping Jacko is by Jonno with the annual argument over who calls in the bat toss. Timmo takes the sunscreen back and squeezes a few globs straight onto Tamie's back.

'Oooh,' she purrs and shivers with each drop. 'Just move the bikini strap around if ya need.'

Timmo's hands move slowly over Tamie's back. The

sunscreen glides across her silky skin. The white cream quickly disappears with each stroke. Timmo rubs across her left shoulder and over the top of her small Southern Cross tattoo. The delicate points of the stars barely mark out more than tiny, proud dots on her skin.

'Oi, Timmo,' Jonno calls out. Timmo jumps and retracts his hand. 'We're about to start. You in?'

'Nah, not yet, I'll jump in later. I'm just gunna quickly unlock the house and check that everything's there.'

'We're doing teams. You're on Jonno's side when ya get back, he chose to bat first. Can ya chuck my voddie into the freezer while you're up there?'

'No worries.' Timmo turns back to Tamie. 'Do you need anything put inside while I'm up there?'

'Nah thanks. It's all in the Esky or the car and I'll crash wherever I fall tonight. Should be right until tomorrow. Cheers for the rub down, we should do it again sometime,' Tamie adds before lying back on her towel.

Timmo brushes himself off and heads up toward his dad's beach house. The sun blares down on his back as he heaves himself over the sand and to the edge of the property. The neighbour's barbecue is already smoking up with some old fogeys holding beers while slapping meat down onto the grill. Some poofta in Speedos saunters around the far house next to the scrub. He drags a trestle table out to the centre of their veranda while mincing away to some imaginary musical.

Mark

'Morning Mark,' his manager greets him when he enters the break room. Mark's crumpled uniform crackles at the arm as he lifts his espresso coffee. 'Well still only just morning. Get much sleep last night? I sweltered.'

'Same here, but I was so knackered I could've slept through an earthquake,' Mark says. He pushes his bag into his locker. 'Ah crap I forgot my badge again. Have we still got the spares?'

'Yeah, next to the microwave.'

Mark grabs the Tupperware box of name tags and browses through the selection. The plastic cards click against each other in a whorl of names of former Ash's Supermarket employees.

'Well, looks like today I'm AJ. Was that a guy or girl?'

'A girl I think. She was only here for a couple of months. She didn't get past the trial period, she couldn't handle the mopping in the evenings.'

'I think I remember her. She was the one who spilt water from the mop bucket on the floor and then spent half an hour cleaning it up with tissues she grabbed off the shelf?'

'Ha yeah. That's the one.' His manager glares down at his watch. 'Time to get back to it I suppose. The float isn't going to replace itself. I've popped you on meats to start with today.'

'Ah crap. Why would you do that?'

'Greg asked for help putting stuff out. Head Office has lowered the price to compete with Cottonvalue and the meat has just taken off, today being Australia Day and all. Most of the shelves were empty last I looked.'

'But we filled them last night. Bugger. I should've taken the day off. Then I'd be at the beach.'

'Yeah, but then you wouldn't be earning shitloads of money working double time while enjoying my fine company.'

Keith

'G'day Uncle Jim,' the mayor holds his hand out for a firm shake.

'How's it going, Keith? You must be stinking in that,' Uncle Jim says, looking at the flowing mayoral robes.

'I am. Can't wait for the formalities to end and to get out of this gear. Aunty May,' Keith nods to an older woman as she approaches the pair. 'Heck of a day for it. Everything looks like it's coming together nicely.'

Keith glances around at the transformed town square. The large patch of lawn is bordered by rows of white pavilions and loaded with food and information stalls. People are starting to gather for the Survival Day events and marking their territory for the day under any available shade with picnic blankets. Later in the day the new beachfront apartments and the town hall next to the square will provide ample shade across half the square. Until then people cram together and suffer the heat to get the most out of their public holiday.

Under the memorial pine final preparations are put into the children's entertainment. The bouncy castle has its first little customers bouncing along giggling. The petting farm awaits the final section of fence to be installed before the animals will be placed on display.

NOTHING WILL BE THE SAME AGAIN WHEN HOMETOWN RETURNS. THE EARTHQUAKE DESTROYED THE HOMETOWN DINER WITH ALL YOUR FAVOURITE CHARACTERS TRAPPED INSIDE. NOT EVERYONE WILL MAKE IT OUT ALIVE.
ONLY THREE MORE SLEEPS UNTIL ALL THE AN-SWERS FROM THIS SEASON'S EPIC CLIFF HANGER WILL BE REVEALED. FIND OUT WHO COMES HOME AND WHO GOES AWAY.
HOMETOWN, RECOMMENCING WEEKDAYS 6PM FROM JANUARY 29.

'No bar this year?' Keith asks.

'Nah,' May replies. 'Hard to get past liquor licensing these days. Couldn't be bothered and we don't have to worry about putting up that ugly fence like last year. Is Dot going to make it in today?'

'Maybe. She's checking all of the water out on the farm and tidying up a bit and then she'll see how she feels. I reckon she'll pop in about lunch time if she comes in. Have you seen that new journalist anywhere?' Keith asks.

'Ya mean Edward?' Jim responds.

'Yeah that's the one. I thought he'd be here to take photos. Only met him once. I think he's only been here for a week, hasn't he?'

'Something like that. Nice kid though. He's over by the flagpoles waiting for the speeches to start.'

Keith turns to spot the pimply twenty-something shift uncomfortably under the flagpole. Sweat stains have already soaked into half of his business shirt. Over one arm a large camera swings precariously. On the other an overstuffed bag dangles with note pads and a voice recorder protruding from the top, ready for when Edward needs to pounce.

'No worries. Should we get this started then?' Keith offers. 'I have a citizenship ceremony in twenty minutes.'

'Sure. I'll get the boys ready for the welcome to country,' Jim says. 'We've moved your speech to straight after so you can duck off straight away.'

'Cheers mate, appreciate it,' Keith says as Jim limps off to find his grandchildren who will perform the ceremony. Keith pulls at his robes to ease a little air against his skin. His CFS beeper vibrates in his pocket and releases several quick sharp bleeps. Keith digs quickly into his pants pocket and pulls out the small black device. He presses on the centre button to switch the noise off and squints to read the message on the screen.

— Extreme fire warning. High alert for all emergency personnel —

'No shit,' Keith mutters to himself. 'It's supposed to get above forty and gusty, of course we're going to be on alert today.'

He places the beeper back into his pocket, adjusts his robe and walks over to the flagpoles ready for the formalities.

Interruption: The passionate ramblings of a man excitedly narrating an event employees use as an excuse to openly drink at work before noon

'And they're off and racing. Goodness Gracious has bolted from the blocks and taken a half yard lead on the field. Sunrise Sunshine is hot on her tail with Tremendous Fortitude galloping steadily behind them. The favourite, Destiny's Infant Love, has stumbled at the gates. She's still in the race but it's hard to see how the favoured mare could sprint back into the competition from such a bad start.

'Mary Wonderful and Sugary Snippets are hot to trot and making gains at the first turn. This truly is a race to behold. The pack holds firm. No clear leader is making any gains. Goodness Gracious still has a slight lead but this is anyone's race. I don't think anyone has been on the edge of the seats like this since the race of 1964 when Polka Donna took the race for her forth cup in a row, making her owners very rich indeed.

'And Oh My Blessed has snuck up from the rear of the

pack. She is creeping up on Caramello as they reach the second turn. No wait. That burst seems to be wearing her down. It is still anyone's race now as they reach the final bend.

'I don't believe it, Hungry Montage has fallen. The two-year-old mare is crashing across the field and taking out most of the pack. She's surely broken a leg in that fall. We'll be lucky if no other beasts are maimed. Six, seven, no twelve animals by my count have tumbled into the grass. It's an unpleasant scene to behold. The jockeys are writhing as much as the horses to get back onto their feet.

'Oh wow no one expected this. What A Bum has bolted from the end of the pack and is challenging Sunrise Sunshine for the lead. This is now a two horse race. The pack will fight it out for third. The American Sunrise Sunshine seems to have worn herself out. She's galloping steady but she's not making any gains. What A Bum, the Aussie, is making this a cup to remember. They're just onto the final stretch. What A Bum still has ground to make up but not all is lost.

'The race is still on. What A Bum is still on the rush to the finish line. She snaps at the heels of Sunrise Sunshine with Julius Candlestick right up there in the mix. I don't believe it. What A Bum, the Australian contender, has found some extra fight in her. One hundred metres out and What A Bum is making a break for it. She's going to do it. The Aussie mare is going to take it all the way from the back.

History is about to be made in this comeback. I've never seen anything quite like it. They're nearing the finish line. Twenty metres to go and What A Bum is going to cross the line a winner.

'AAANNDD she made it. What A Bum has taken out the cup. I don't believe it. A real come-from-behind victory. She deserves it. There's no doubt that spectacular fall casts a shadow over today's race and surely an inquiry will follow, but this moment belongs to What A Bum. What A Bum has achieved a tremendous feat today, taken home a coveted national trophy, and made her owners very happy.'

PART II

'Good afternoon. This is Cassandra Cummings with your midday 5CCB news update.

'The Bureau of Meteorology has increased today's maximum forecast with the mercury already tipping over the forty degree mark. The rise in temperature and the prediction of gusty winds has authorities on high alert. Police Commissioner Darren Stymes has released a warning that any firebugs caught setting blazes will be prosecuted to the full extent of the law.

'Looking at local news and a record number of tourists and beachgoers are expected in Founders Bay for the Australia Day holiday. Authorities are reminding people to drink responsibly and take care out on the beaches and in the sun. The northern waters off Founders Bay have been declared a no go zone due to the sudden influx of bluebottles.

'Today, Founders Bay will also welcome twenty-eight new citizens, who will make their pledges in the Town Hall shortly. Also in the Town Hall today is the Australia Day

Awards ceremony and charity barbecue hosted by Mayor Keith MacDonald.

'In sports, local athlete Dwayne Story has qualified for the Beer Pong World Championships. The local footy star kicked one hundred goals for his tenth season in a row and says that the change of code is a challenging and rewarding experience for him.

'Sunny and forty-three today. I'm Cassandra Cummings. I will return for the next 5CCB news update in an hour.'

Helen

Margaret steps out onto the veranda and places the punch onto the kids' table. She looks around at the three seats.

'Helen, why don't you push the extra seats onto the one table?' Margaret asks. 'There's only the three kids this year.'

'Tradition I guess,' Helen responds. 'Besides, they'll all be on their phones the whole time and off down to the beach as soon as lunch is over. Would you like some more wine, Aunt Liz?'

'Yes please dear,' she answers. 'You wouldn't happen to have any of that nice shiraz we drank last year. You know the one. It sucked my cheeks right in on the first sip.'

'I think we might in the garage. Hold on one minute.' Helen straightens and looks out to where Grant, Arthur, Rodney and Zac are laughing around the barbecue with beers in hand. 'Grant,' she calls out. The boys keep laughing. 'Grant!'

'Don't bother dear,' Liz says. 'Once the men start talking business there's no getting a word in edgeways.'

'You're right Aunt Liz. I'll just duck into the garage and see if I can find it. Margaret can you watch the potato bake for a minute. The oven should start beeping soon.'

Margaret nods as she sips on her chardonnay. Helen sighs and heads back into the house and toward the garage door. She clasps the cold handle and pushes the door open. A waft of oil and sweat creeps into her nostrils. She waves her hand across her nose before walking to the back corner of the garage. She sighs again.

ANOTHER D-LIST CELEBRITY HAS JUMPED ONTO THE SEX TAPE BANDWAGON. SUNRISE BLOSSOM, A POPULAR VLOGGER, HAS BEEN EXPOSED ON ALL FOURS WHEN HER EX-BOYFRIEND RELEASED A SEX TAPE THE PAIR MADE TOGETHER. BLOSSOM ADMITS SHE STARS IN THE SEX TAPE AND SAYS SHE WILL BE TAKING ALL LEGAL AVENUES POSSIBLE TO RECEIVE COMPENSATION FOR THE RELEASE OF A PRIVATE VIDEO. OR AT LEAST ROYALTIES. VISIT WWW.CELEBSDOWNUNDER.COM.AU FOR ALL THE LATEST CELEBRITY GOSSIP.

Helen

A whimpering escapes from the shadows of the garage.

'Oh god, I forgot you're still here.' Helen spits at the snivelling coming from the corner. She marches on to the wine fridge and pulls open the door.

The whimpers soften. A metal chain rattles on the cement floor. A cold nose nudges Helen on the leg.

'Ew, no,' Helen commands. 'I told you to stay away from me.'

She swings her foot and feels a smug satisfaction when it connects. Whimpers and scuttling noises retreat to the darkest corner of the room.

'Disgusting dog. You're far too old you know. I don't know why Grant insists on keeping you.'

Helen turns to the fridge door and fingers her way through various labels. The coolness of the bottles caresses the tip of her fingers as she runs over each bit of glass.

'Here we are. Barossa Reserve Shiraz,' she reads. 'Last bottle. Aunt Liz had better enjoy it.'

Timmo

'HOWZAT?!' the fielders celebrate.

'Howzat nothing,' Jonno fires back.

'C'mon mate, it's easily LBW,' Timmo says. 'We'll go to

the third ump. Tamie, that was out wasn't it?'

Tamie looks up from the towel where she is sunbaking with her two girlfriends.

'Sure, why not,' she says indifferently.

'Fuck off! You weren't even watching,' Jonno swears. 'Screw this game. I'm gonna find some lunch.'

'Good idea. It's about that time,' Timmo says. 'I've opened the house if anyone wants to dump their stuff in there,' Timmo offers to deaf ears.

'Fish'n'chips then?' Jacko says, throwing his bat onto the sand. 'Is the place just off the town square still open? I love their chicken salt. Oi, Tamie.'

'What?' She replies without moving.

'You want anything from the fish'n'chip shop?'

'A chicko roll would be great.'

'Make that two,' Karen adds.

'Me too thanks,' Caitlin throws in as well, lifting herself slightly off her towel. She pushes her sunnies up to reveal an already stark tan line around where the frames had been. 'D'ya reckon you could get us some coke while ya there? I need a mixer.'

'Fine. Anything else ya highnesses want? Hope you guys know ya paying for yer own grub.' Jacko hisses. He looks over his shoulder. 'Any you boys coming to grab some food as well? Make one trip and then hit the coldies again.'

'Nah cob,' a few of them answer back. The rest fiddle with their drinks and iPhones. Two start playing music from their phones, and competing Hottest One Hundred frequencies blare from tiny speakers.

Jacko eyes the crowd suspiciously. 'I reckon they're just gunna nick some of ours, the cheap cunts,' he mumbles.

'Where's my flag?' he adds. His eyes dart around the sand until he spots his half-buried Aussie flag next to his Esky. He pulls roughly on the fabric. The empty tinnies jangle together as they tumble from the flag onto the sand. Jacko whips the flag in the air to dislodge the coarse grains, and ties it around his neck as a cape. Jacko, Jonno and Timmo turn and head off toward the centre of town. 'Where's yours?' Jacko asks.

'In the car still. I'll grab it later,' Jonno says.

'Which one you got?'

'Boxing kangaroo.'

'Nice. That's what the Aussie flag should be. When are we gunna have a vote on it? Where's your flag, Timmo?'

'Threw it out,' he answers.

'What the fuck, man? Where's your pride?'

'Last year you used it as a cum rag. It was covered in jizz, Bundy, and probably bernardi stains—I saw some of those chicks you were hooking up with. I wasn't washing that shit. It's probably still in the wheelie bin here unless someone else thought enough to put it out for collection.'

'Gross, man,' Jonno says.

'Gross but awesome,' Jacko states. 'I lost count of how many times I came last year. Must have been that E you got

48

us. It gave me a rager for the whole weekend.'

Jonno bursts into a fit of laughter.

'What the hell man?' Jacko asks.

'More of a V than an E,' Jonno sniggers, grasping his stomach in an effort to compose himself. 'You must've got the Viagras. Jezza and I were playing pill roulette and forgot to tell anyone else.' He stumbles into another fit of laughter.

'Ya cunt!' Jacko punches Jonno in the arm with a thud. Timmo snickers to himself as the pair trade blows for the length of their trek across the beach.

Each grain of sand scorches their bare feet as they walk along. A pair of kids giggle as they dash erratically in front of them in their escape to the cool water, trailed by their mother's shrill directions to swim between the flags. The glare off the surface renders the ground near-white and painful to look at.

'Ah fuck!' Jonno bellows, oblivious to the mother's gasp of indignation as he hops about, his knee wrapped in his hands. He looks up to see the rusted frame of the lifeguard's tower he'd just kicked.

'A little early to be running into stuff, mate,' the lifeguard warns from his perch, his bright red Speedos and cap bobbling with laughter.

'Ya right mate?' Timmo asks while Jonno calms down through intelligible mutters.

'Yeah mate. It's nuthin'. I'll walk it off.' He straightens his leg and presses down on it tentatively. He grimaces. A tear forms in the corner of one eye.

'You sure you right mate?'

'Yeah. It was nuffin'. Just a bump,' he squeaks as he limps on.

The sand continues to sear their feet as they walk towards the dilapidated jetty. A couple of retirees sit in deck chairs at the end of the rotting wooden frame. They remain as immobile as the rods hanging over the edge of the steel rail, lines limp in their impotence. They barely move even to speak or sip from their tinnies, they just stare out to sea.

Ronald

'Thanks Doctor Harry for that important story on keeping your family happy and healthy. Doctor Doctor will be back on your screens next week. This is Ronald Ray with your Today's Affairs update. Everyday Australians are sick and tired of bureaucracy getting in the way of everything these days and disrupting our day-to-day lives.

'Tonight, John Symonds investigates an exclusive story for Today's Affairs, which brings to light the sheer reluctance of local government officials when it comes to cooperating with their state and federal colleagues. His investigation into citizenship ceremonies uncovers how much the role of local government overlaps state and federal jurisdictions, and their cover-up in an effort just to remain relevant. Here's John with more.'

'Scandal in the town halls. But not the usual affairs between staff. This scandal sits rightly in the hands of every council mayor in the country and their refusal to streamline citizenship ceremonies.

'State and federal governments want to slash red tape and ballooning costs by streamlining citizenship ceremonies. The proposal would see all proceedings digitised through Skype and WhatsApp with a central official to officiate the ceremonies live from Melbourne. The proposal removes the costs of catering and venue hire, frees up local officials to focus on the needs of their constituents, and with this added flexibility allows ceremonies to be conducted from the comfort of new citizens' homes on the government's new and improved NBN service.

'We spoke to several district council mayors. One mayor said "citizenship ceremonies are important local events for the new members of our community". Another said "no official proposal has been received but we will allow all appropriate consideration of proposals from our friends in state and federal parliament". Another emailed exclusively to Today's Affairs. "We are not concerned with the minimal costs of citizenship ceremonies, as they are paid for by donations and run by volunteers who generously donate their time".

'As you can see, local councils are flippantly unconcerned about spending taxpayers' money on the rising costs of citizenship ceremonies. They are more concerned with maintaining their own status within the community. This is John Symonds for Today's Affairs. Back to you Ronald.'

'Thanks John. Scandalous. It's outrageous that local government officials are only out to protect their own jobs. Tune in at seven-thirty tonight for the full story and more. I'm Ronald Ray, see you tonight.'

SINGER ROSS JONES MARRIED HIS BOYFRIEND OF TWENTY YEARS TODAY IN A PRIVATE CEREMONY. THE COUPLE SAY THEY ARE INCREDIBLY EXCITED TO SHARE THEIR COMMITMENT WITH THOSE CLOSEST TO THEM. THE NEWLYWEDS WOULD NOT REVEAL DETAILS AS THE EXCLUSIVE PHOTO SHOOT AND INTERVIEW WILL FEATURE IN FEBRUARY'S EDITION OF WOMEN'S FORTNIGHTLY, AVAILABLE MONDAY.

Jane and Danielle

'Have you got any booze up here with you?' Jane complains to Danielle.

'No, my parents have stashed it all in the garage, but we aren't allowed in there,' Danielle says. 'Mum and dad have locked it and don't let the keys out of their sight. I can't believe they're so paranoid about me drinking.'

'Oh good, I didn't want to rain on your parade if you'd scored something better.'

Jane reaches into her bikini and slides out a bladder full of liquid. Her breast size shrinks noticeably to a sporty B-cup. Danielle's mouth gapes at the sight of the clear alcohol. She remains speechless as Jane awkwardly tugs out a second bladder from her other cup. The liquid in the second sack is a sickly orange colour.

'Why do you think I needed a hot pink bikini? No one notices anything else through the fluro and if anyone does stare I bitch them out.'

'But your boobs have always been big.' Danielle points in wonder at the sudden breast deflation. She places her hands under her own and squeezes gently. 'I always thought you were bigger than me.'

'Ah yes, but I'm committed to my alcoholism, so I have to maintain the illusion. I first learnt this trick sneaking booze into concerts. They started cracking down on BYO, but if they reached for the girls I'd just scream rape and they'd leave me well alone. So... screwdrivers? Sorry it's a bit warm but it's better than nothing.'

Timmo

'Fuckin' muzzos,' Jacko curses as they look across the open town square. 'It's bad enough they're here for our jobs and now they have to take over the town for their own Sharia party.'

Giggling kids bounce across the yellow and blue inflated castle. Some squat outside fenced enclosures to pat small farm animals and some native species. A man stands with a snake wrapped around his arm, the children watching his every move. Hundreds of people stroll between the pavilions in the square, several pushing prams while taking swigs out of two litre water bottles.

'Yeah, what is it this time?' Jonno adds. 'Why do they need their own party on our fuckin' day of pride?! If they were real Australians that's what they'd be celebrating.'

'Go back to where ya came from!' Jacko shouts over the increasing wind. No one turns to acknowledge him.

'Yeah. If you don't want to join and do it our way then fuck off back to your own country!' Jonno yells.

Timmo walks silently, scanning the square for the neon flashes of the sign of the fish'n'chip shop. He decides not to point out to his less tolerant mates the numerous banners printed with 'Survival Day' and the flag sporting a yellow circle on a red and black background that dominates the flagpoles in the corner of the square. Instead he locks on to a very welcome 'open' sign hanging in a window, and quickens his pace.

'Oi wait up,' Jonno calls out. Jacko and Jonno rush forward to catch up with Timmo.

'What's the rush mate?'

'Fuckin' hungry,' Timmo says, his eyes still set determinedly forward.

Keith

'I would also like to finish by once again paying my respect and acknowledge the traditional custodians of the land on which this meeting takes place and also pay respect to Elders both past and present. I on behalf of the local council, honour the Elders past and present and thank them for welcoming us to their land. Thank you also to Uncle Jim, who performed such a warm welcome to country, and remains such a vibrant and upstanding member of our community and enthusiastic advocate for First Nations peoples.'

Mayor Keith MacDonald steps down from the small stage. *That can never be said too many times*, he thinks to himself. A small applause follows him off the podium. He holds out his hand to Uncle Jim for a firm shake and photo opportunity. The camera flashes and clicks rapidly. Uncle Jim releases and returns to the microphone to continue with proceedings.

'Thank you, that should do it,' Edward says with a

nervous twitch. He looks down at his watch. 'I must duck off, I want to catch the start of the citizenship ceremony.' He pauses in the middle of rapidly loading his pens and voice recorder back into his bag and looks at the mayor, 'Isn't that where you're supposed to be right now?'. The camera drops suddenly from Edward's grip and bungies on the neck strap. 'Thank god for small miracles,' he stutters. He pulls the camera up and shuffles it into its case while stepping rapidly toward the town hall.

'I suppose that's my cue,' Keith whispers to himself.

The mayoral robes drag roughly over the grass as he follows Edward to the town hall. Edward darts away from him quickly, his gait an odd leap mashed together with some attempt at a controlled walk. His collection of equipment bashes heavily against bony hips with each stride.

'Once again, thank you to Mayor Keith MacDonald for opening the Survival Day commemorations,' Uncle Jim's voice over the PA is little more than a crackle by the time Keith reaches the splintering wooden door of the town hall, trailing completely into the background when Keith enters the town hall. Keith pauses for a moment to caress the fading polish. Sharp lumps press against his callused hands.

'You just need a bit of love and care. I know I've neglected you in my twenty years, but I promise to do something once the budget allows for it,' he says to the Town Hall.

A familiar if weary voice in his ear drags him back to more pressing obligations.

'When you retire you can do all of that sort of thing,' Dot admonishes him, Keith's next mayoral robe in hand. 'Right now you need to hurry up and change. Everyone is in the hall waiting for you.'

'I'm coming, I'm coming. Why are you here so early?' Keith says as he tries to escape from his current robes and shuffle into the fresh ones and at the same time follow his wife through the musty foyer into the main hall.

'I finished tidying up and watering so I thought I'd whip up some éclairs for the CWA table for after the ceremony,' Dot chattered away. 'New Australians always seem to be so fond of my pastries.'

Their mismatched steps echo across the roughly polished floors. On all sides the walls haunt them with black and white photos of the early settlers. Fading eyes watch them as they push through concertina doors.

Rows of folding chairs block the direct route to the elevated slabs of wood that was all the town hall could manage for a stage. A lonely microphone is mounted precariously at the centre of the stage. The cord tangles down the pole and across to a single speaker.

'Go on quickly,' Dot insists. 'Some of them look a bit nervous. They've been here for a while. I think they're very excited about today.'

'Yes yes, I'm on it,' Keith says. He reaches into his pocket and pulls out a crumpled piece of paper. He smooths it hurriedly to reveal the running sheet for the citizenship ceremony. He reads his lines. 'Welcome, presiding officer duties, pledges, bit of a chat and then... the goddam national anthem again, already. That is not a tune meant to be heard more than once. I'll be eagerly voting for a new one by the end of the day.'

> Absolutely soaked in sunscreen. Feel like I'm swimming already and I haven't even hit the water yet.
>
> 30 people like this

Mark

'Cheers,' Mark says to Millie as he accepts his double shot coffee. 'I really need this.'

'Second one today,' she replies. 'Not many people want coffee in this heat.' Her café polo shirt waves loosely and falls back into place once she hands over the coffee. 'Long day for you?'

'Long week. I'm filling in for whoever didn't show today on top of my own shifts.'

'God, that would suck. Just think of the money and the

fact that we get to close at five today. Heading to the beach after?'

'Dunno. Depends how I feel. Might just be a few beers in the backyard.' He sips his coffee. His eyelids flutter as the coffee caresses his throat. 'That's just what I needed. Back to it, I guess. Message me if something's happening tonight, I might feel like a binge. That's if I can still move by the end of my shift.'

'No worries, catchya.'

Mark steps out of the café and into the main plaza of the shopping centre. He pauses to enjoy his coffee. The warmth is soothing in his tired state, while the caffeine fires sparks of energy down his spine.

Something feels odd to Mark as he stands in the corridor readying himself again for work. Something has changed, but he can't quite work out what. He spins around, absorbing everything he can as he looks about. His place of employment stares down its rival supermarket from across the central plaza of the shopping centre, glaring lights and discount arranged aggressively. Mark shakes his head as he spots the difference, Cottonvalue have lowered their meat prices, again, and displayed them in mobile fridges out the front of the store to take advantage of last minute shoppers clamouring for barbeque fodder. A few workers are only just finishing the final touches.

'Head Office called,' Mark mimics to himself, 'they want all the prices lower and much *easier* for guests to access.'

He takes another swig of his coffee and heads back into the store to find his manager has switched him to the soft drink aisle.

'Ten bucks says the nightfill guys are all pissed on the beach,' Mark sighs to himself.

Keith

Keith sighs loudly as he sits next to Dot, glad to be finished with all the polite chatting after the citizenship ceremony.

'It's incredible what some of them have been through to get here,' he mutters so only his wife can hear. 'I couldn't talk any more about all those horrible ordeals with that one family at the end.'

'I know what you mean dear,' Dot replies. 'That lovely Afghani couple, over there. They spent four years in detention. Such a horrendous experience for them to go through. And they had no contact with their families until they arrived here. That lovely lady that works in the council's cultural office...'

'Carol,' Keith interrupts.

'Yes that's her, Carol. She only just got them in contact with her brother again. He's the only one left from home. The others are all dead or missing. Horrible, *horrible* stuff.'

'It's too much, dear. I much prefer just to think about how much we benefit from having them here, otherwise I know I'll crack listening to all the tragedy they've survived through. The Filipinos who came through in the last batch have done wonders with the CFS, we now have several enthusiastic young men who can drive the emergency firetruck and round-the-clock volunteers.'

The national anthem echoes throughout the town hall and drowns out their conversation.

'Bugger,' Keith groans.

'That would be the Australia Day awards ceremony starting,' Dot reminds him. 'You'd better dash off,' she adds, passing over his final robe for the day.

'Right you are, dear.' He leans in and pecks his wife on the cheek. 'I'll see you after. I hope there's some éclairs in the fridge at home. I always miss out on refreshments when I officiate at events.'

Keith ducks from the room. He shuffles quickly across the musty foyer to the council meeting rooms, again juggling himself into new robes. The door swings open easily across the carpeted floor. The pale, faded weave muffles the sound of his arrival. He eases the door shut and straightens for the end of Advance Australia Fair.

Simon

'Claire, you remember Sam, Thomas, Other Sam, Michael and Matt,' Simon says.

'Yes I do,' Claire says, nodding as the assortment of men shuffle into the room. Each bends down to give her a kiss on the cheek, or in the vicinity at least, and a hug to Simon and Tony. They all make a point of offloading their Bollinger and Grange bottles for Simon to serve up. 'No Declan this year?'

Sam drops his head. 'Declan and I are no longer an item,' he says, kicking off his thongs.

'Oh, I'm so sorry,' Claire says. 'How long were you together?'

'Six years,' he replies.

'A lifetime in gay years,' Other Sam snaps in. 'Most of us don't hold onto a relationship through the season.' He flops his sneakers next to Sam's and unloads some flutes from the cupboard. 'Bolly, anyone?'

ARE YOU TIRED OF SCRUBBING AT BATHROOM SCUM AND FEELING LIKE YOU GET NOWHERE? ARE YOU SORE AFTER HOURS OF BACKBREAKING TOIL JUST TO GET THE SHOWER TO THE LEVEL OF CLEAN YOU NEED JUST TO FEEL WHOLE AS A WIFE? TAKE THE PAIN AND FRUSTRATION OUT OF CLEANING THE BATHROOM WITH THE NEW, IMPROVED SMACK! POWER CLEANER. WITH SMACK!'S REVOLUTIONARY NOZZLE YOU CAN SPRAY EVERY SURFACE WITH

OUR ALL NATURAL ANTI-BACTERIAL FORMULA
WITH EASE. JUST SPRAY AND IN FIVE MINUTES
THE GRIME WILL JUST RINSE AWAY, GIVING YOU
MORE TIME TO SPEND WITH YOUR FAMILY. SMACK!
IS SO EASY TO USE THAT EVEN YOUR HUSBAND
COULD DO THE CLEANING. SMACK! POWER CLEANER.
AVAILABLE NOW IN ALL BOTH SUPERMARKETS.

Simon

'What sort of question is that sweetheart?' Matt remarks. 'Of course Bolly. Bubbles is always appropriate.'

'Okay then,' Other Sam says. 'Any objections to Bolly?'

'Oh, I'm not sure David will do champagne,' Claire says.

'David you say?' Thomas is intrigued. 'He's here again this year? We didn't scare him off?'

'Yes, he's back with his review of your performances last year,' Claire pauses. Apprehensive faces await her next words. 'I'm joking. He's setting the table or something with Tony.'

'Darl, you're such a blast,' Michael says, hauling his vodka and tequila bottles onto the kitchen counter. 'Is there space in the freezer, Simon?'

'Attempt to find some if you're game, but it's your funeral,' Simon laughs. 'As they say at that filthy club, The Milky Bar, if you can get it in then it fits. Food's nearly ready everyone, get out to the table. There's some snacky bits there already. Cheeses and whatnot.'

'Praise Cheeses!'

'I won't be a sec with the mains,' Simon continues. 'Claire, could you please give me a hand with the salad?'

'Sure,' Claire says as the men grab their glasses and wander out to the crowded dining room.

'Claire, catch,' Simon says. He throws a crystal bowl of green salad at her. Claire snaps around and marks the bowl against her chest.

'One day I'm going to drop one of your precious bowls.'

'They're just bowls. I tend not to dwell on broken bits of crystal when it comes paired with the prospect of buying a new one,' Simon says casually.

Simon takes the lead, a hot pot of curry in hand, and heads straight for the dining table.

'Whop, whop, whop, whop,' the table of men chime at the sight of Simon's pink oven mitts. David shoots Claire a confused glare.

'Zoidberg,' Claire mouths over the noise.

'It smells delicious,' Thomas proclaims merrily. 'You've outdone yourself again, Simon. You've got room for everyone to sleep tonight, right, when we can't move anymore because you've stuffed us too full of food and wine?'

'Sure. Plenty. I'll pull out the futons, and anyone who doesn't fit can camp on the beach. It's going to be a lovely balmy night.'

The conversation cheerfully proceeds through the standard catch up stage. David strokes Claire's leg and flirtingly tempts her with more wine. His face drops to allow for the widest puppy-dog eyes he's able to muster.

'Darling boy, how cute,' Michael blurts out. 'You breeders can be adorable when you want to be.'

'Michael!' Simon glares. 'He's still fresh. Don't pounce just yet.'

'Fresh? What does that mean?' David asks.

'He just means you're still new at the table,' Claire slips in, 'and so everyone still needs to play nice. So Matt, how's the legal practice going? Any interesting cases?'

'Here we go,' Tony throws his hands up.

Matt places his fork down and presses a napkin to his mouth.

'As a matter of fact,' he says, pushing a stray hair back into place. 'We did have one the other day that you wouldn't believe. You can't make this stuff up. As usual I can't tell you any identifying info, but the juicy details more than make up for that. Most of it is already in the papers anyway, not that they can get much right. This one lady tried to poison a cheating husband but failed miserably. It was a fuck-up on par with that case I told you about using the wrong acid to dispose of the body case. It was a fizzer.'

'What the hell, Matt?' Tony says. 'Too soon.'

'Never too soon for a joke to lighten the mood,' Other Sam says. 'I demand to be entertained.'

'Anyway,' Matt continues. 'She'd been sneaking White King into his coffee every time she made him one. Not enough for him to taste it but at three cups before work and three cups after she fed him quite a bit of bleach over time. And she did this for months, I'm not joking, months. A few drops at a time, for months thinking it would work.'

'What? How did he not taste that?' Michael asks.

'He wanted to consider himself a "modern husband", probably to make up for the cheating, so made sure he did the shopping every week. He also did a lot of the cleaning and noticed that the White King kept being moved. So in the grand tradition of modern respectful husbands, he decided to install cheap security cameras from eBay around the kitchen, dining and bathrooms to see how it was being used and by whom. Don't ask me why that's the first logical step, but that's what he did.'

'The bathroom? How could it be okay to film that?' Claire asks, her jaw stuck in a perplexed gape.

'I told you it was ridiculous. That's the end of the story for the husband. The camera footage showed the wife pipetting tiny amounts of cleaner into his coffee so he took it to the police and a divorce lawyer.'

'Natural response,' Tony threw into the conversation.

'Yes, and the wife was arrested for attempted bodily harm. Of course it could have been attempted murder but intent wasn't produced in a prosecutable way.'

'Just attempted? It was bloody obvious bodily harm,'

Michael shouts, swigging from his wine glass.

'Wait for it. That's the best bit.' Matt laughs. His hand reaches for his glass to quell his chortle. 'It was only attempted harm because this "modern husband" in his quest to be ecologically friendly had started buying plant-based, chemical-free cleaners. And the wife didn't seem to bother reading any of the labels—she said in her statement she thought it was just rebranding. So all the husband got in the end was a few doses of eucalyptus oil.' The table explodes in hysterics.

'Impossible,' Michael splutters.

'It sounds like an urban legend,' David says.

'This table is full of urban legends,' Claire whispers. 'Uncle Simon survived a home invasion at his last place, even though he was tied up, beaten and shot in the leg.'

'What?' David gasps, 'I thought that was just a joke.'

'Nah, haven't you seen the scar on his leg?'

'Well, yes. I just assumed he'd made up a more interesting story for it,' David whispers back.

'It was fifteen years ago, but it was real. See? Urban legends.'

'And—and, here's the kicker,' Matt gasps between gulps of Moët. 'The husband ended up going away for longer than the wife who tried to kill him.'

'What? How?' Simon asks.

'Because of the cameras in the bathroom,' Matt answers. 'He recorded lots of other footage of his wife doing stuff

like singing and talking to herself and distributed copies
of it without his wife's permission, so was convicted under
privacy laws.'

The table falls into a portrait of silent, gaping mouths.

Helen

'Kids. Lunch,' Helen calls up the stairwell. She doesn't hear
any movement from upstairs. 'Kids. Now!' her voice turns
to the screech only a mother can muster.

Footsteps drag across the floor on the second level.

'Everything is set at your table,' Helen adds as the kids
walk past her. 'And make sure you reapply sunscreen twenty
minutes before disappearing after lunch. You'll need it on a
day like today.'

'We need it any sort of day,' Danielle slurs. 'That's what
they said at school. The UV is just as bad when it's cold and
cloudy.'

'That's why it's good that you wear hats all year round,'
Helen rebuffs.

The girls ignore Helen and slink out the sliding door to
their three person table in the corner of the veranda.

Helen ponders for a moment trying to spot what's
different about Jane, then disregards it with a flick of her
hair and pulls back her shoulders in preparation for her
entrance back onto the terrace. She collects the last bowl

of bush-herbed macadamias on the way and steps out into the hot shade of the outdoor dining space. The men have cornered themselves at one end of the table while Margaret and Aunt Liz sit across from each other at the other end, leaving the final seat at the head of the table for Helen.

Helen drags out the wooden seat and places the bowl of nuts on the table.

'Please, help yourselves everyone,' she announces feebly. The men have already loaded their plates with kebabs, chicken and marinated steaks.

'Sit down, Helen,' Aunt Liz pats her on the arm. 'The men are talking Test results. You won't get through to them in that state.'

'Bloody hell,' Margaret blurts. 'Are they still going on about that? That was at Christmas. It's been a whole month since they had their arses handed to them by the Poms. Who cares about that now? We'll get the ashes back next year, if they're clever enough to drop Watson as captain.'

'Careful Maggie,' Aunt Liz warned. 'They'll convert you without you knowing. You sound like you're already half way there. This is a fantastic drop, Helen dear. Whereabouts did you get it?'

'From the Barossa, I think. Grant picked it up on one of his work trips. I don't think you can get that vintage anymore though. You might be able to pick some up at Dan Murphy's if you search for it but they've sold the last of it at the cellar door.'

'Oh Helen, I didn't compliment you on the dress earlier,' Margaret says. 'It's absolutely lovely and looks very light. It must be great in this weather. Although, it's actually not too hot in the shade here. Is that new work there on the house?'

'I'm taking credit for that one,' Helen says. 'See those extra shade cloths and fans up there.' She points to the corner of the veranda. 'They block the direct sunlight from this level. Above that I had some solar panels installed so that they can use the direct light that was such a problem in the kitchen. We also leave the northern top window open in the corridor upstairs. It just sucks the hot air straight up the stairs and out the house.'

'Ingenious, Helen.'

'If only there was more consistent rain here. We could throw in a couple of water tanks and cut ourselves off the grid. The price of having utilities connected is just astounding these days.'

TODAY ONLY! GET INTO ASH'S SUPERMARKET TO RECEIVE HUGE AUSTRALIA DAY DISCOUNTS. ASH'S WON'T BE BEATEN ON PRICE. IF YOU FIND A COMPARABLE PRODUCT FOR A LOWER PRICE ELSEWHERE WE WILL REFUND YOU FIFTY PERCENT OF THE COST. COME INTO ASH'S TODAY FOR ONCE-A-YEAR AUSTRALIA DAY SPECIAL OFFERS.

Helen

'Tell me about it, with all that electrical nonsense,' Aunt Liz says. 'Your Uncle Philip bought one of those plasma screen televisions off Gumtree. It sucks the absolute power out of the house. He yells at me just for using the dryer when it's bucketing down and cold but doesn't understand the cost of his own technology addiction.'

'Men, right,' Margaret adds into the conversation. 'Don't get in the way of their goddam gadgets or sports.'

'Language, Margaret,' Aunt Liz hisses.

'Sorry Aunt Liz.'

'Never mind, Margaret. I know exactly what you mean. Grant makes all these impulse buys. I won't lie, I do *really* enjoy some when they arrive but others I'm bored of almost immediately, like all that garden equipment that just lies around taking up space. You can hire people to do those things for you and they don't clutter up your shed. It's not that hard.'

Claire and David

David rubs his jaw. It aches quite a lot. He hasn't been able to keep his mouth from hanging open much at all through the entire lunchtime conversation.

'I don't see what the big deal is,' Sam continues, 'it's my

body and I can do what I want with it after I'm dead.'

'Oh, it's a bit much,' Tony wails. 'Even for you.'

'I'm just saying that I should be allowed to donate my body to necrophiliacs if I want to,' Sam insists.

David chokes on his champagne. The idea isn't any easier to swallow the second time around. 'So you're telling me that you're keen to find some dead guy and just fuck him?'

'What!? It doesn't interest me in the slightest,' Sam is taken aback. 'I've just had the good fortune to be able to get off in a lot of inventive ways, which I'm very grateful for. But not everyone is that lucky. Certainly not necrophiliacs—they never get the chance to have sex in the way they want to, even though it doesn't really hurt anyone. So it's my way of doing something good in the world, by letting a necrophiliac have his way with me after I'm gone.'

'I don't want to seem judgemental of your gay lifestyle or anything,' David wrinkles his nose in disgust. 'But dude, that's gross.'

'Not to mention very illegal,' Matt chimes in. 'When you die you become a thing, property that belongs to the state. You're not a person anymore, so you can't give consent to sex. And the consent you're giving now becomes null and void. It's pretty much the same reason bestiality is illegal. Animals aren't able to give consent either.'

'Hah!' David is suddenly interested in the conversation again, pleased that he has a story to contribute. 'It's like that kid from school. Chook-fucker George!'

'Oh my!' Sam and Tony both exclaim, though with very different expressions on their face.

'That's horrible, David,' Claire chides, not at all impressed with his contribution. 'I can't imagine the trauma that poor chicken must have gone through.'

'Oh, when did you become a PETA freedom fighter?' David retorts. 'Besides, it didn't feel a thing. I heard it was a roast chook his mum had bought at Ash's.'

'Ugh, I can't imagine how that's any better.'

'Well actually,' Matt says, looking thoughtful, 'all your friend Chook-fucker George did was stick his cock in a meal, not an animal. I'm sure his mother wasn't real happy about it, but it's not animal cruelty, as far as the law is concerned.'

'Come off it! It's perverted and unnatural.'

'David, my darling boy,' Michael leers, 'you can imagine the view this table might take on some straight man's beliefs about what's perverted and unnatural.'

'Fuck, I'm sorry,' David backpedals. 'But you can't seriously expect me to believe that having sex with a dead person is illegal, and having sex with an animal is illegal, but that having sex with a dead animal is not illegal.'

'Actually David, I think that's exactly what I'm telling you,' Matt confirms.

'Well there you go Sam,' Tony chortles delightedly, 'if you're going to fuck a guy, make sure he's alive, and if you're going to fuck an animal, make sure it's dead!'

'Phew,' Claire wraps it up, 'I think we've definitely set a new standard for dinner conversation.'

'Fuck, how do you know all this stuff?' David exclaims.

'I'm a lawyer,' Matt explains. 'Plus I'm gay. Gays have been persecuted before. Know thine enemy, which unfortunately includes the law. And don't even get me started on religion.'

'Aren't you an atheist?'

'Exactly.'

CHRISTMAS IS COMING AROUND AGAIN. IT'S NEVER TOO EARLY TO PREPARE WITH OUR CHRISTMAS SPECIAL PACKAGES. COME IN STORE TO FIND HUGE DISCOUNTS ON ALL GIFTS AND CHRISTMAS SUPPLIES. YOU'LL FIND EVERYTHING YOU NEED AT GOOD PRICES TO KEEP YOUR FAMILY HAPPY AT CHRISTMAS. ASH-MART DEPARTMENT STORES. OPEN EVERY DAY EIGHT AM TO NINE PM.

Timmo

'The munchies are fading now,' Jonno announces as he exits the fish'n'chip shop. 'I reckon we got ripped off. That brew was light.'

'True dat,' Jacko says. 'I'm gunna have to light up again already. Too early for the other stuff. Gotta keep it away from you, Jonny-boy, to make sure little Jonny doesn't end up fuckin' someone else's girl.'

'Fuck off mate, you weren't even together anymore,' Jonno fires back. 'I can fuck whoever I want. And besides, all the chicks are single this year.'

'I think Buds and Striper are kinda together,' Timmo chips in.

'Nothing that sticks,' Jonno says. 'They're only together for about half an hour after a shit-ton of piss.'

Jacko's attention is drawn from the beach to the celebrations in the town square.

'Bloody hell, they're still at it,' Jacko says while blowing on a chip. He nods up toward the mass of tents and people.

'Check out the firies just standing around,' Jonno comments as they swagger past the town square again. Jacko dips his hand back into the greasy plastic bag to sneak out more chicken-salt-laden chips. Over in the square two firefighters chat casually with bottles of water in hand. 'Can't they smell that smoke? Shouldn't they be doing something about that?'

'What smoke?' Timmo asks. 'I can't smell any.'

'I can,' Jacko says, a chip hanging like a ciggy between his lips. 'Smells like bushfire.'

'There,' Jonno points to the base of the flagpoles, where a small wooden bowl holds the embers of a fire, the source of the white smoke curling up towards the flags and drifting away. 'What the fuck is that?'

'Dunno,' Timmo says. 'Some traditional thing?'

'Probably why the firies are here. They're waiting for it to go out completely. Unlucky buggers can't just piss on it and fuck off home,' Jonno says.

'Why the fuck would someone do that? Just throw water on it.' Jacko yells to the crowd. 'No one in this country lights fires in summer you bastards.' He flings a chip high up toward the town square. It lands with a flop on the head of an old woman standing by a small stall. She twists around and waves a brown arm at the lads.

'Why would you fuckin' do that?' Timmo curses, as he retreats towards their site on the beach, Jacko and Jonno quick on his heels.

'Fuckin' muzzos deserve it,' Jonno grumbles.

Jane and Danielle

'God I hate how they talk about us like we aren't even here,' Jane complains. She takes a sip of her punch, cringing through the sweetness.

'I just hate that we're not on the adults table,' Danielle adds. 'It's not even like we've got a huge family. We could all easily fit on that table.'

'Empty nest phobia,' Nicholas explains. 'They just don't want to accept that their children are growing up. We're all teenagers now, so they're hanging on to the last childlike moments before you disappear off to uni.'

'You might be going to uni,' Jane says. 'Once I finish high school I'm on the next plane or boat out of this country.'

'Where will you go?' Danielle vocally dreams with Jane.

'I dunno, Greece, America, New Zealand. It could be Tasmania for all I care. Just as long as it's away from this place. I'm sick of it. I'm sick of the rules.'

'Tasmania is still Australia,' Nicholas corrects.

'Still overseas,' Jane retorts.

'Yeah, shut up nerd,' Danielle teases.

'You shut up.'

'Kids, knock it off,' Helen calls without turning her head. 'Once you've finished your plates you can head off and do what you want. Just get along until then.'

'Yes mum.'

'Yes Aunty Helen.'

All three glance down at their minute steaks, chicken, potato salad and coleslaw, picking at the food with little interest.

INTRODUCING THE MAMMOTH FOUR-BY-FOUR TRADE UTE. IT'S THE TOUGHEST VEHICLE ON THE MARKET WITH A HUGE FIVE TONNE TRAY AND

LOADS OF INDESTRUCTIBLE HORSE POWER. IT'S
THE WORK TRUCK EVERY MAN AND TRADIE NEEDS
WITH EXTRA-LARGE CUP HOLDERS IN THE CAB AND
SPACE FOR MAN'S BEST FRIEND IN THE BACK.
THERE'S ROOM ENOUGH FOR EVERY TOOL YOU OWN
IN THIS BEAST OF A MACHINE. GET YOURS NOW
FOR THE AWESOME PRICE OF $99,990, DRIVE AWAY.
MAMMOTH. THE TOUGHEST WORK VEHICLE ANY
MAN WILL FIND.

Jane and Danielle

'This food sucks,' Jane whispers. 'Your dad always overdoes the meat.'

'I know,' Danielle leans toward her conspiratorially. 'We let him think he's a legend at it, but he always gets distracted and lets it go too long. I'm surprised mum's never cracked it at him.'

'Just drown it in sauce,' Nicholas passes her the Rosella bottle.

'Cheers, cuz,' Jane snatches the bottle. 'Anyway, my friends from school have already been overseas. Their parents took them but they got to do whatever they wanted. It's so unfair. They loaded Facebook with all their pictures. I'm so jealous. Trish spent the September holidays scuba diving in the Maldives.'

78

'That's an actual place?' Danielle slurs a little.

'Of course it is,' Nicholas states. He shoves a sausage in bread into his mouth. 'It's a country,' he mumbles. Sauce seeps between his lips.

'I know that, nerd. I just always thought that Getaway just oversold it and that it was just a set up.'

'Nah Dani,' Jane says. Her eyes widen eagerly. 'It's real, and it's so beautiful and free there. One day I'm going to be there. Straight after year twelve I'm off. Fuck schoolies. I'm going to Rome or as far away as Jetstar can get me.'

'Language, Jane!' Margaret hisses absentmindedly, her attention focused on the wine glass in front of her. She leans to Helen's ear, 'Sometimes I'd be happy to post her there myself.'

'Heard that mum,' Jane rolls her eyes.

'Well it's true. If you put your mind to it you could be an honours student like Nicholas.' Margaret takes a sip of her riesling. Jane sticks her tongue out at the back of her mother's head. 'I saw that, dear.'

Jane sulks around to face her cousins again and glares at Nicholas.

'What?' Nicholas shrugs. 'It's not my fault you two set the bar so low at school. The teachers love me.'

'Teacher's pet. I'm just glad I'm older,' Danielle says. 'If they'd expected me to follow your example, they would have been disappointed.'

'Exactly,' Jane says.

The trio sit in silence among their creamy salads, Christmas themed paper plates and plastic cutlery. *It's either a trust issue*, Danielle thinks, *or mum is still trying to use up the serviettes she bought five years ago.*

'I'm done,' Jane declares. 'Can we go now?'

'As long as you've all finished,' Helen answers.

Danielle and Nicholas shove the last remnants of coleslaw into their mouths and grunt to signal completion of their meals.

'Very well.'

The trio drag their wooden seats across the pavers and ready themselves for the dash down to the beach.

'Hold on a second,' Helen interrupts their escape. 'Slip, slop, slap and slide,' she recites.

'Mum, we're not twelve anymore,' Danielle retorts.

'Where are your rash vests?' Helen asks.

'I'm too old for a rashie, mum,' Danielle complains.

'That's wonderful, Danielle. So then you'll also be old enough to pay for all the medical bills for your cancer treatment when you get a melanoma.'

'I will, actually. Next year I'll get a part-time job and pay for all my treatment,' Danielle snarls in a wave of rolling sarcasm.

'You won't give me that lip when I'm holding your hand so Dr Dowelling can cut out a mole.'

'Mum, there's no moles that need cutting. I've checked myself and so does Dr Dowelling once a year.'

'Fine, just don't get burnt,' Helen concedes. The trio of teens march down to the beach. Helen opens her mouth to protest.

Helen

As soon as the teens are out of sight Helen seizes the opportunity to confront Grant. She stands, grabbing the empty chardonnay bottle as she does.

'Grant,' she says calmly to no response. 'Grant,' she hisses. The men's conversation cuts out to focus on Helen. 'Could you please help me in the kitchen for a moment. I don't think I can lift the mixer to whip the cream for the pavlova.'

'Sure honey,' he says, following her into the air-conditioned coolness of their tiled kitchen. 'Where is it?' He asks once the door shuts behind him.

'I don't need your help with that,' Helen shakes her head. 'We both know I'm the stronger of the two of us, I can lift the mixer myself. What is that *thing* doing here?' she shakes her hand toward the garage door. 'I thought you were putting him up for adoption, not bringing him with us on holidays.' Her eyes darken.

'Love... but... honey... but...'

'No buts. You promised me you would get rid of him. What happened to the ad you put on Gumtree?'

'I got a few calls about him,' he stammers. He bends down

to pull out the benchtop mixer.

'A few? Why isn't he gone then?' Helen's eyes narrow.

'I just want to make sure he goes to a good home. We shouldn't rush this, sweetheart. And most people are like us when we were looking. They prefer young pets.'

'I want him gone. Do you understand?'

'Yes dear.'

'God help you if he messes up anything in the garage, or the kids see him. You will have to get rid of him *today*. Have I made myself clear?'

'Yes dear.'

'Now go back out to your mates. They seem so lost without you,' Helen nods to the outside table. The four men stare awkwardly between their beers and the reflected glare of the sun on the water.

'Yes dear.'

Interval: The day Tilda dared speak up during interventions on operational matters under the green hill

Men line themselves around the table. Their numbers have all come up but they know this time there can be only one winner. Stacks of chips spread across the table to show the weight behind each bet.

Kingston stands at the front of the table controlling the crowd. He can see the uncomfortable sways of the men as they squeeze together ready for the final spin.

'Any tea or coffee, loves?' Tilda asks from the edge of the crowd.

No one notices Tilda. She senses the tension in the room and pushes her drinks trolley toward the door.

HAVE YOU PLACED YOUR BET IN TODAY'S RACES?
MISSED OUT ON THAT SURE THING BECAUSE
OF QUEUES? JUMP THE QUEUE WITH THE NEW

'Right men,' Kingston begins. 'We all know the stakes. We all know the rules. Let's get this underway.'

Kingston spins the wheel and releases the ball into the fray. The tapping of the ball with each movement flicks apprehension and anticipation into the men's eyes. They watch, eagerly awaiting the outcome. Kingston glares steadily at each of them ready to call out any cheats amongst them. He spots crossed fingers, men rubbing their thumbs over a rosary cross and muttering to themselves. *All in order*, he thinks to himself.

The wheel begins to slow. Resignation appears on the faces of half the room as they realise their bets have missed the mark. The ball pauses on its number. Cheers and grumbles erupt through the room. Hands are thrown out eagerly to shake with the victor's despite the lack of an official ruling.

Kingston clears his throat. Attention falls upon him.

'Congratulations Reginald,' he announces. 'It is your

turn to be Prime Minister. See you all again next week.'

Kingston removes the ball from the table and exits through the side door before anyone calls for party unity.

PART III

'Good afternoon. This is Cassandra Cummings with your 5CCB new update.

'Straight to regional news, and local athlete Dwayne Story has received the Coonawarren District Australian of the Year Award for his outstanding efforts with the local football team and his athletic representation of our country overseas. In awarding the accolade Mayor Keith MacDonald said "I have known Dwayne since before he was born. He and his family have always made a contribution to the community as we know it".

'In other news, NRL Australian captain Cameron Davis has taken out the National Australian of the Year Award for his work encouraging rural Indigenous children to participate in the NRL code. This week's Prime Minister stated "Cameron has been an outstanding captain for all Australian sports fans, and I hope to be a captain to lead Team Australia just like Davo has done for our national rugby team".

'To weather, the Bureau of Meteorology has continued

catastrophic fire warnings and reminds everyone out in the sun today to take all precautions and slip, slop, slap and slide.

'I'm Cassandra Cummings. I'll be back in the next hour for the next Australia Day 5CCB news update.'

Keith

Keith sighs in relief after the Australia Day Awards as he heaves the livery collar and robe over his head and hangs it over the town hall kitchen chair next to him. The metal clinks against the frame of the chair. A fleck of gold drifts off the collar and onto the carpet to join the layers of dust collecting on the floor.

'What a joke. Dwayne flamin' Story.' Keith mutters to his wife as she tidies up a few lime-green cups and saucers. 'All he did was kick a few goals and get on the piss.'

'I know dear, but he was the only one to submit a nomination.' Dot hands Keith another soap-covered teacup, the brown crack that traces the length of the handle a testament to its resilience to thousands of users over the years.

IT'S THAT TIME OF YEAR, BACK TO SCHOOL TIME. ARE YOU READY? ALL YOUR BACK TO SCHOOL

Keith

'He did his own nomination and signed it his bloody self,' Keith hisses, continuing his rant. 'What about those immigrants from the citizenship ceremony. They escaped a life of persecution and torture to come here and clean toilets and wash trucks. That's a true Aussie battler. They would've spent half, if not more of their lives locked up, and yet they get here and work harder to contribute to the community than that Story kid.' Keith pulls at the collar of his suit. 'So am I done for the day?'

'Yes you are. The formalities are over, anyway,' Dot confirms. 'There's still just a few of these dishes to dry and then you're free.'

'Thank god for that,' Keith sighs. As if triggered by some

morbid cue, the CFS beeper in his pocket bleeps urgently.

'Is that another warning, dear? You should add more hospital funding to your next election campaign,' Dot advises as she lifts the livery collar from the chair and begins to curl it away. Keith peers down at the beeper.

'No love, it's a fire. Just a bit of smoke reported way south of home,' Keith reports. 'I'd better get to the station and onto it before the wind really kicks in.'

'Okay darl,' Dot replies. She steps up to peck Keith on the cheek. 'Just be quick luv. It would be nice to see you for dinner this year.'

'I'll be home as quick as I can. It might just be some young dickheads playing with fireworks like last year. Though I would've thought they'd learn. Sarge has been onto them and confiscated every cracker he could sniff out—thankfully wankers like that like to brag, which makes his job a little easier. One day, once they grow up and have their own family, I hope they learn not to mess around like that during fire season.'

Ronald

'Good afternoon, this is Ronald Ray with your Today's Affairs news brief. Amongst tonight's exclusives is footage of violent scenes at the bowser in response to the sudden rise of petrol prices at most Ash's and Cottonvalue franchised petrol stations. Sandra Tomtoms has more.'

'Thanks Ronald. Outrage has broken out at the sudden twenty cent jump in prices by dominating petrol outlet owners Ash's and Cottonvalue.

'In a Today's Affairs exclusive we have the reactions of everyday Australians to the sudden hike.

'I asked true blue Australian families what they think of the skyrocketing prices. Most are appalled at the impact these extra costs will have on their family budget. Others are calling on the government to intervene to protect working families from bankruptcy.

'How this is affecting every family is shocking. Back to you Ronald in the studio.'

'Outrageous, thanks Sandra. We'll have this incredible story plus many more exclusives tonight at seven-thirty. This is Ronald Ray. Stay tuned.'

Mark

'What's going on?' Mark asks his manager from the front of

the store. He looks out into the shopping centre at a bain-marie being wheeled into the entrance of Cottonvalue. An Asian couple with a much younger woman push the bulky food warmer into the store. Their spare hands are loaded with Eskies and green bags.

'Is that Sora and Akari? From the Japanese restaurant down the road? And is that their new waitress?'

'Fuck, it is,' his manager curses. 'What are they doing here? It looks like they have their full spring fair kit out today. Damn it!' he hisses, looking across at his Cottonvalue counterpart. The Cottonvalue manager brushes imaginary dust from his crisp green uniform as he ushers Akari and Sora through the checkouts. The couple start to set up the bain-marie near the entrance. The Cottonvalue manager shakes Sora's hand and smiles. From under his arm he pulls out a sign and walks out to place it on the sandwich board in the plaza space.

'Free fucking sushi!?' Mark's manager fumes as he reads the sign. 'I didn't think they could stoop any lower than what they did earlier.'

'You mean the two-dollar trays of premium barbecue meat?'

'Yeah that. There's no way we can compete with that.'

'Duty manager, you have a call on line three, duty manager,' the PA crackles.

'Can you stay here for a sec?' Mark's manager asks. 'Keep an eye out for any more changes they make while I'm gone.'

'No worries,' Mark says.

Mark folds his arms and watches the sushi prep. Sora, Akari and their waitress swiftly move in automatic motions around their work space. Within minutes they have several rows of sushi rolls lined up and begin offering them to customers walking through the door.

Mark

Mark looks toward the supermarket exit. A few customers juggle a handful of samples along with their bags of premade salads and bottles of coke and sarsaparilla. Mark glances over to the customers across the plaza wandering out with free homemade gelato in one hand while struggling with a canvas shopping bag loaded with chips, soft drinks and deli goods in the other. Mark shakes his head at the sight.

'That was Head Office again,' Mark's manager whispers conspiratorially. 'They've caught wind of how much free food Cottonvalue is offering and now they want us to increase our giveaways.'

'What? How are we expected to do that and stay on budget?' Mark asks. 'Between the two supermarkets we've already contracted half the restaurants in town to serve up food.'

'I guess we could get Coonawarren Takeaway to do us some fish and chips to go with the gelato.'

'Sheez, how much is that going to cost us?'

'We could probably spare a couple grand for it. Oh and you need to get back to it and put all the fifty percent signs out.'

'Fifty percent! Freakin' half price. What the hell?'

'Head Office wants to outstrip Cottonvalue's sales and prices on Australia Day. You better be quick about it. I've already tweeted it on our local Twitter account.'

Mark rolls his eyes, which his manager ignores. Mark walks to the office where the stash of blank labels resides.

Timmo

Tamie lays just beyond the shade of her marquee, lapping up the unobstructed rays. A sudden shadow looms above her. The instant coolness is a refreshing coat on her skin.

'Here's your Chicko Rolls,' Jonno says, dumping the plastic bag next to her and her girlfriends. 'No promises on the chips. I reckon Jacko ate 'em all.'

'Fuck off,' Jacko says. 'I only ate like fuckin' five.'

'Five bags,' Timmo fires out. Tamie snickers with her hand over her mouth.

'Cheers guys,' she announces. She takes the sweating plastic bag and shares out the Chicko Rolls. 'Anyone want sauce? There's like five things of them in here.'

'Yeah, and they were like two bucks each so someone better have them,' Jacko whinges.

Timmo

'Where are you guys going?' Tamie asks as the boys start to walk back up the dune.

'Just up to the house for a minute,' Timmo answers. 'We're gonna blast the aircon for a sec while we finish eating.'

'I'll join you. Aircon sounds great.'

Karen and Caitlin swap smirks and lie back down, Chicko Rolls perched in hand.

Jonno and Jacko bicker about the Kokoda-like hike to the fish'n'chip shop as they stroll up the dune to the car park. Timmo lags behind as his feet struggle through the pull of the sand. Timmo forces his eyes up to the yard of the beach house, a square patch of lawn fronted by a strip of succulents, scuttling with lizards. He sighs at the sight of the flimsy wire fencing that has no hope of keeping out the wildlife, yet somehow convinces people to walk the long way around. The plucky reptiles will stubbornly hold their spot to bathe in the sunlight until someone gets almost close enough to touch them.

Timmo drags his feet up to the cement access ramp. The relief of solid ground is short-lived as his soles start to burn, and he hastily hobbles up the ramp, clumps of sand clinging doggedly to his legs and feet.

'Hang on guys,' he says. 'Wash your feet out here. There's no tap at the back door.'

Timmo hurries to catch up with Tamie as she gets to the beach shower. The cement block around the drain is splattered with sand surrounding a neutral zone of pooled water, which Timmo gratefully steps into.

'Thanks for the rescue, Timmo,' Tamie says, 'I just had to get out of there. Karen and Caitlin have spent the last forty minutes on the pros and cons of an epilator.'

'I get that,' Timmo says. He nods towards Jacko and Jonno bickering as they grab their stuff out of the boot. 'They spent the past hour switching between the cons of muzzos and the pros of box gap.'

'Ha!' Tamie shrieks. 'You win.'

'Hurrah!' Timmo cheers gloomily. He yanks on the single tap of the beach shower and shoves his foot under the squirting water.

'Fuck!' Timmo shouts, retracting his foot and rubbing at it as he hops around. 'The water's boiling.'

'Let it run for a bit,' Tamie suggests. 'It's the same at home. The cold tap burns in a heatwave.'

Jacko and Jonno duck off towards the house. Jacko quickly unties his flag from his throat and dumps it onto his car as they pass by. Tamie turns to engage with Timmo.

'Why do you hang out with those guys, anyway?' she asks. 'You're much smarter than them. And less douche-y'.

Tamie and Timmo flick the remaining drops of water off their almost clean feet and head after Jacko and Jonno.

'I dunno,' Timmo responds. 'I guess they're my oldest friends. I've known them since kindy.'

'So? You don't have to hang around with them anymore.'

'Well, I do until I move closer to the city for uni. I can't be arsed with the two-hour each way trip,' Timmo says. He slides back the glass door. A cool blast of stale air rushes past them.

'God it feels so nice in here. No heat. It must have been closed up for ages.'

'Probably since this time last year. Dad has been overseas a lot.'

'How depressing. This is a great place and your dad never uses it for anything?' Tamie says. 'So what are you going to do at uni?'

'Well, don't tell the guys but I'm going to study engineering. I've scored all the classes I wanted as well.'

'Why wouldn't you tell them?'

'Cos they thought I was always partying and flunking with them through high school. But school was always easy for me and engineering sounds like fun.'

'Sounds like a lot of fun,' Tamie jibes.

'What would you know about engineering degrees?'

'I've heard they're the biggest pissheads at university. If someone isn't hospitalised on one of their pub crawls it's a shit night out.'

Timmo leads Tammie into the house. Blue tiles cover the entire floor in a dated attempt to emulate the ocean.

'Are you sure you could keep up with them engineering students in full swing?' Tamie pokes Timmo in the ribs. 'After all, you're adult entry now. You're a bit over the hill.'

Timmo snatches her hand and pokes her back. Tamie squeals and slaps at his hand, her ability to fend him off ruined by ticklish spasms. Timmo keeps poking, and brings in his spare hand in to invade her other side.

'Cough,' Jacko states from the doorway. 'Don't mean to break up this little party.'

Timmo and Tamie snap apart. Tamie's face blushes a deeper shade of red over her burning face. Jacko walks across the cold tiles and switches on the light. The unnatural brightness flashes through the open living and kitchen space.

'This place is still lovely,' Tamie diverts the conversation. 'Has anything changed since last year?'

'I don't think so,' Timmo says. He walks over to the fridge and opens the door. The light flicks on and cold air rushes out. 'It's all working. I don't think dad has been here in years. Or he has but leaves everything the exact same way he finds it.'

'Shotgun the master bedroom,' Jonno says, darting up the stairs with a Quicksilver bag in hand. The bag slaps dramatically against the wall as he swings around the corners.

'Fuck off mate,' Jacko chases after him. 'I get it this year. You're just going to pass out on the beach again anyway.'

Their shouts become muffled as they reach the corner of the master bedroom. Tamie walks over to the kitchen to join Timmo by the sink in search of drinking water. She takes a bite out of her Chicko Roll and cringes.

'Gross, soggy already,' she complains. 'I hate plastic bags. How long did it take you guys to walk back? It didn't seem like you were gone that long.'

'To you maybe. Jonno and Jacko were distracted by the Survival Day ceremony and felt the need to loiter for a while.'

'I can imagine how that went.' Tamie takes another bite out of her Chicko Roll. Timmo cocks his head at Tamie, his eyes glistening a questioning look. 'What? It would be wrong to waste it just because it's not as fresh as it oughtta be.'

Timmo turns away to hunt out a glass. Murmured yelps come from the top of the stairs. Timmo fills his glass up from the sink and takes a swig. He spits the liquid straight down the sink.

'Ew,' Tamie laughs.

'Freakin' salty bore crap. Why can't they have the good ol' chlorinated stuff like the rest of the country?' Timmo remarks.

'Fuckin' give it back,' Jacko shouts from the top of the stairs.

'I fuckin' found it, it's mine,' Jonno spits back.

The pair reach the bottom of the stairs before Jacko tackles Jonno to the ground. His shoulder smacks on the nearby couch, pushing it and the rug a metre closer to the wall. Tamie rolls her eyes and takes another nibble of the Chicko Roll. She cringes again but keeps eating all the same. Jonno wriggles under the weight of Jacko's bear hug. The pair grunt and roll across the pale floor. Jonno pulls out a little blue plastic bag and holds it as far away from Jacko as possible. They heave and groan as they push and grip at each other's bodies.

'What the fuck, guys?' Timmo walks over and snatches the plastic bag out of Jonno's hand. He holds it up to the light and sees a pinch of tiny crystals through the plastic. He squints closer at it, not recognising the contents.

'So, you're sure that your dad ain't been here in a while, huh?' Jacko says, hauling himself up off the floor. 'I don't remember seeing that last year.' Jacko nods toward the plastic. His left hand remains clenched into a loose fist.

'What is it?' Tamie moves her head close to Timmo to join him in squinting at the plastic bag.

'How do you not know what that is?' Jacko uncurls his fist. A glass pipe stained black around the bowl sits in his hand. 'It's fuckin' ice. And it definitely wasn't here last year, otherwise it would be gone already.'

'Druggo,' Jonno spits.

'I only know what's good. And besides, it's Straya Day and I'm on Team Straya. So we get to let loose and celebrate the freedoms we have in this freakin' awesome country. It's un-Strayan not to. It's what our founding fathers would have wanted.'

'Yeah, 'cos it's un-Australian to not be off your tits on ice. Dude, I'm sticking to pot and piss,' Timmo says.

'Is that like crystal meth? 'Cos not even once, mate,' Tamie asks.

'Nah mate this is ice. Different thing altogether,' Jacko answers.

HAVE YOU BEEN INJURED AT WORK? CONTACT
THE TEAM OF LAWYERS AT MARSHALL&MARSHALL

Timmo

Jonno snatches the blue bag and jumps onto the couch. He stretches the end of the blue plastic until he rips a small hole in the end. He inserts a finger into the gap and pulls out a pinch of crystals for the pipe.

'Must you do that inside?' Timmo asks.

'Well, I bloody can't do it outside, the pigs are out in force today. And I bet your old man does it inside. Sure you don't want some?'

Timmo shakes his head. Jacko hisses and launches himself toward the couch next to Jonno.

'Don't offer me none or nuffin', fucker,' he says.

'Why the hell would I?' Jonno teases.

Jacko holds up his cigarette lighter and dangles it just out of Jonno's reach. Jacko takes a swipe, but redirects its swing to slap his hand down on the bag of ice. A few crystals slip out of the bag and disappear between the couch cushions.

Jacko returns to glaring at Jonno who waits for a bargain to be made.

'Are you guys going to get those?' Timmo asks and points at the couch.

'Get what?' Jacko answers.

'The ice that fell down the couch? Dad will know it was us if he finds it.'

'Relax mate. If your dad does this stuff he wouldn't know it wasn't him.'

'Fine, you can go first,' Jonno glares at Jacko.

Jonno holds out the pipe. Jacko smiles and bops his head along to an imagined beat. He bounces his hand slowly closer and closer to the pipe before plucking it out of Jonno's hand. The pair fall back onto the couch and fire up the cigarette lighter. The small flame flickers under the bowl, and within moments a white smoke rises from the crystals. Jacko puts the end of the pipe in his mouth and inhales deeply. The smoke rushes through the pipe into his mouth. He falls back on the couch holding it in, while offering pipe and lighter. Jonno snatches at them and repeats the process. The pair lie back on the couch, their mouths shut and eyes bulging. Jacko coughs first. White smoke escapes between his lips with each gasp for air. Jonno smiles. His lips part. A trail of white floats out in a steady stream, the smoke curling up toward the ceiling.

Tamie squints down at the smoke. Curiosity flashes in her eyes. She walks over to the pipe in Jacko's hand and takes a whiff of the rising white fumes. She inhales as if searching for an odour.

'Smells like nothing,' she says. 'I would have thought it would stink.'

'It's pure.' Jacko fires upright. His eyes widen in a burst of energy. 'It's so fuckin' pure. My skin is sparkin.''

'It's fuckin' electricity,' Jonno jolts in his seat. The rush begins to consume him.

Tamie's nose twitches. Her eyes spark alight. A primal glint sneaks onto her face.

'Um, Timmo,' she whispers. 'I think we better leave these two alone.'

She grabs onto Timmo's hand and leads him toward the stairs. Jonno and Jacko start twitching and bopping in their own world. Wave after wave of a heady rush snap Jacko to a standing position. He starts running around the couch, smacking the edge rapidly as he does.

The dusty smell of the upper level engulfs Timmo as he's dragged upstairs. He's quickly distracted from the antics below by Tamie's nails sinking into the skin of his hand. She spots a bedroom and throws Timmo inside.

'Wait, what are we doing? I don't think it's safe to leave those two down there.' Timmo says. He freezes in the middle of the room.

Tamie stands in front of him and quickly yanks off her bikini top. The velcro rips on her boardies as she tears open the fly. She pushes her bikini bottoms and boardies down in a single motion. Timmo yelps as she stands back up to reveal a hairless, toned body. Her small nipples are framed by a white triangle of tan lines, matched by the pale stripe tracing the line of her g-string line over her hips. She drops to her knees in front of Timmo and rips at his shorts. Barely seconds pass before Timmo is hard in her mouth. He moans in an ecstasy of his own. Tamie pulls back quickly.

'I totally want to do this. I reckon I'm high and I haven't fucked you yet,' she sighs.

Tamie latches onto Timmo's arm. In an unnatural show of strength she pulls him to the carpet and mounts him. She thrusts down onto Timmo with sharp control. She rises slowly and pushes down onto his cock again. She repeats the same motion. Sweat beads over her body as she increases the speed of her movements. They grunt and writhe to encourage each other. The spasms in their muscles fire intensely to a quick climax.

Tamie shuts her eyes and exhales her release. Groans and barks rumble beneath her. She looks down between her legs at Timmo partially lying in a juicy mess.

'There's no need for all of that,' she purrs.

'No need for what?'

The groans echo underneath them again.

'What the hell is that?' Timmo asks.

'Sounds painful. One of them losing it and in strife?'

Tamie jumps off Timmo and quickly dresses. Timmo struggles to his feet. He pulls feebly at his boardies still wrapped around his ankles. He straightens the velcro away from his deflating knob and gently presses on the fly. He chases after Tamie, who's already down the stairs beyond Timmo's sight. The groans echo fiercely at the top of the stairs, and then a gasp of pain shrieks below him. Timmo sprints down the stairs, heart suddenly pounding again.

At the foot of the stairs Timmo runs into Tamie, stopped frozen in awe at something in the living room. Timmo looks up, his face matching Tamie's stare. A display of rough fucking is on show before them. Jacko holds the back of Jonno's wife beater in his hand, pulling as he thrusts aggressively into Jonno's arse. Jacko spits down onto his groin to lube his dick, a hysterical grin of pleasure plastered on his face. Jonno moans with each plunge, jerking furiously at his prick with one hand.

The pair spasm suddenly in preparation for climax. They shudder and release simultaneously.

'What the fuck man?' Timmo yells instinctively. Jacko and Jonno snap their heads around and stare intensely, their eyes lurching out of their sockets. 'Not on my dad's couch. Clean that shit up.' The pair on the couch remain motionless.

'Well—um—so—,' Tamie stutters. Jacko remains with his groin flush against Jonno's arse. 'I think I'm ready to go for a dip again. How about you, Timmo?'

'Uh-huh, yep. I think I'm ready too.'

Tamie and Timmo step tentatively toward the door.

Jonno and Jacko's heads turn steadily following each step. The door slides shut behind Timmo. The pair blink at the sudden light and shared acknowledgement of the insanity they had just witnessed inside. With each quick step back toward the beach, their disbelief dissipates into uncontrollable splutters of laughter.

'I never thought,' Tamie says through her hysterics, 'when I slept with all Jacko's mates to get back at him that he'd try to do the same thing.'

Grant

The metal spatula scrapes through the grease of the barbecue. Grant wipes the sweat from his forehead that appears with each push forward. He drags the pile of grease and fat to the corner of the barbecue plate. In a steady motion he flicks the black muck over the edge and onto the dead grass below.

'That was a bloody good feed,' Zac says, patting his stomach with his spare hand. The other holds a bottle of Crown nestled in a stubby holder.

'Bloody oath, mate,' Rodney echoes. 'That chook was spot on. What did you use to marinate that one?'

'Just a little secret recipe found in the Masterfoods prepacked marinade section,' Grant gloats.

'Grant dear,' Helen calls from the porch. Her white dress

waves as crisply as the beginning of the day. 'Could you please help me with something in the garage?'

The men all quickly look over their shoulders, then all but Grant snap their necks back to stare aimlessly at the beach. Their expressions mimic school children who have just heard one of their number be called to the principal's office.

'Yes dear,' Grant calls back over his shoulder. He hands the spatula to Rodney and marches up to the veranda to meet his wife.

'This way,' Helen hisses once Grant is within whisper reach. 'He did it again.'

Grant shrinks into his collar. The early warning signs were clear, there's no good news to be found in the garage. Helen leads the way down the stairs. Grant drags his feet, reluctant to go forward but also careful to not make a sound to distract her. A rotten stench wafts up the stairs. Grant shrinks further into himself. Helen marches over to the tool cupboard and spins on the spot. Her finger points determinedly at a dark patch on the cement. A hot pile of brown shit marks the floor. The stench emanates from the mark and fills the room.

'He fucking did it again, Grant. Explain this mess to me, Grant,' Helen demands. A shadow flickers across her eyes.

'Um—well—it's only natural,' Grant stutters. 'He's locked in a garage, where else did you expect him to go?'

He hunches under the commanding presence of his

wife. Her arms start to tense ready for the onslaught. Helen swings a fist suddenly at Grant's chest. The punch smacks the air out of his lungs.

'I know it's natural. I'm just wondering what it's doing here. I told you to get rid of him months ago. I'm growing tired of this.' Helen's eyes darken further.

Grant kneels down on the cold cement. He throws his open palms up to beg of his wife.

'I'm so sorry. I know what you said. I know you wanted him gone.'

'Really? You know I wanted him gone?' Her arm flings back. Grant cowers on the spot. 'He can't, just can't, be here anymore. If you want to keep a pet then we need to start from scratch. Something I can train properly from the start. We have to start over.'

'But, we've had him for so long,' Grant peers through his fingers. His arms shake violently with adrenaline. 'I can't just get rid of him. I've tried. No one else is willing to take on an old boy.'

'Yeah, I'm not surprised.' Helen's shadow shrinks. 'I was sick of him a few years ago.'

'Why didn't you say anything sooner?' Grant rises tentatively to the less threatening posture of his wife.

'I've given you plenty of warning, Grant, but you simply refuse to listen.'

Grant

Helen slaps Grant with the back of her hand, the thwack of the blow resonates off his cheek. Grant stumbles backward in shock. Helen's white dress sways seductively as she repositions herself from the slap. Grant's eyes are captured in the movement of his wife. A sense of thrill and eagerness to please her mingles in with the adrenaline of fear.

'I told you this time last year, and the year before that. You never listen to me. I think we'll need to have some lessons in hearing for you.' Helen folds her arms. Her shoulders rise to loom like a statue over her whimpering husband.

'Do you want to do a listening exercise darling?' Helen purrs.

'Yes dear,' Grant sniffles. He sits himself on the cement cross-legged. His eyes remain focused on the dark patches on the ground.

'Very good. Are you listening now?' she commands.

'Yes dear.' Grant can feel an erection stirring.

'And you know the rules? You must do whatever it is I want.'

'Yes dear.' His cock starts throbbing in his pants.

'Get rid of him. I want him dealt with today. He's not staying here. He's not coming home with us. He needs to be gone.'

'But dear.'

'No buts. You know the rules. You must do this for me.'

'No, it's not refusal. It's just—' Grant stops mid-sentence, distracted by his arousal as he reaches the verge of orgasm.

'Just what?' Helen's arm raises back again. Grant's gaze is fixated on her erect nipples pressing through her dress.

'It's just, how am I supposed to do that, here in this town, on a public holiday?' Grant pleads for more instructions from his wife.

Helen sighs and glances around the garage. She walks over to the toolbox, the glinting metal scrapes heavily across the bench as she pulls it closer to open it. Grant watches in horror as she returns and hands him a hacksaw.

'Dear, no,' he pleads. Helen smacks him again. A chill

runs through him. 'Yes dear.'

'Unless you think of another way to get rid of him, this is what you will do. That's an order. Oh, and clean all of that up. Now, before he eats it.' She points at the shit on the floor.

'Yes dear.'

Helen's lips stretch into a thin smile. She turns, the dress flowing as she spins and marches to the door, her face already falling into a mask of sophistication and gracious hospitality. She clicks the lock on the garage door leaving Grant on the floor, trembling along with his beloved companion, the hacksaw lying in the palm of his hand.

Jane and Danielle

Jane tilts her sunnies to the tip of her nose. Over the rim she inspects two men sitting in deck chairs set up in the water, the waves soaking their shorts and keeping their beer cool. Her perving is interrupted by a dry sucking sound from the towel next to her.

'Looks like we're out of booze,' Danielle says. 'We shoulda flogged some off your mum before we came.'

'Pisshead,' Nicholas teases his sister, tossing a handful of sand at her as punctuation. Danielle squeals and aims a kick in retaliation.

'Shouldn't you be off wanking or whatever else you do

in your room all the time?' Danielle says.

'Shouldn't you be off puking up your lunch?' he snaps back.

'Just piss off, would ya.'

'Fine. Sounds good to me.'

Nicholas stands and brushes himself off, careful to let the breeze blow the sand directly into Danielle's eyes.

'You tool.'

Nicholas jerks his hand back and forth in front of his crotch with a smug open grin as if wanking himself, though the gesture is lost on Danielle as she continues to blink sand out of her eyes. He drops his hand and strolls towards the water to cool down a bit. As Danielle's vision returns she sees Jane smiling and winking at the guys in the deckchairs. Their red flesh glows under their sleeve and neck tattoos. One of them nudges his blond mate on his ink-scrawled back to get his attention.

'What are you doing?' Danielle hisses.

'Getting us that extra booze,' Jane replies without taking her eyes off the two guys. 'No need to freak out.'

'But what if they come over here?' Danielle twists her neck around to look back towards the beach house. The second story balcony is visible over the sand dunes.

'That's the whole point. What's wrong with you? Don't tell me you've still got your V-card.'

'Of course I haven't. I'm not frigid,' Danielle snaps back. 'Just not within view of my parents.'

'Well if these guys give us their booze you'll have to put out for them. You know how it works. If you want more to drink, you may have to suck one of them off.'

'I know,' Danielle cringes.

Jane keeps up her attention on the boys, even throwing in a blown kiss, until the two young blokes take the bait. They grab their chairs and the Esky floating between them and strut towards the beach, water dripping from their boardies. Danielle spots more tattoos on their legs in the shape of almost identical Southern Crosses on the side of their calves.

'Sweet,' Jane says, 'I hope they have Cruisers.'

She straightens up as the guys approach, her boobs pressing out against her bikini top. Danielle remains lying back on her elbows, letting Jane take the lead. The two shadows cast across Danielle's stomach do little to remove the searing heat from her skin. Specks of sand fly across her as the boys come to a complete stop.

'So what are you boys doing here?' Jane greets. She pulls her sunnies off and teases the band with her lips and tongue. 'Do you come here often?'

The blokes swap glances and smutty grins.

'Actually we came here last year,' the blond one says. 'This is our second time. Our mate's dad lets us have the beach house but we mostly just hang out in the car park and on the beach.'

He points up toward the collection of V8s up in the car

park and the adjacent house.

'Doesn't that belong to a governor?' Danielle asks.

'Something like that,' the blond guy continues. 'We were invited by Jacko, who's around here somewhere. His other mate's old man owns the place. I'm Derek by the way. He's Jezza.'

'Hi there,' Jane responds, 'I'm Jane. This is Dani.'

'Are you guys like sisters?' Jeremy asks.

'No silly,' Jane giggles. 'We're cousins.'

'How's about a tinnie?' Derek drops his Esky.

'Absolutely. What's on offer?' Jane raises herself high in a seated position.

'Well, we're on XXXX. You want one?'

'Not straight away,' Jane says flirtatiously. 'Got anything sweeter?'

'I thought you chicks might be after the sweet stuff,' Derek responds. He opens his Esky and rummages through the ice. 'I'm pretty sure there's Breezers in here. At least some Red Bears from last weekend. Ah, there we are.'

Victoriously he retrieves two white Breezers dripping with ice.

'Here you are, girls,' Derek hands them over.

'Actually I'm good with beer if that's on offer,' Danielle says.

Derek and Jezza flash each other dubious glances. Jezza straightens, grabs a XXXX can for Danielle and steps carefully over to her side of the towels.

'Do you girls mind if we throw our stuff down here?'
Jezza suggests.

'Nah, go for it,' Jane says, her hand reaching out for the
Breezer.

Derek pops himself down next to her. Jezza eases himself
down next to Danielle. He holds out the XXXX as his
entrance ticket. Danielle accepts the icy can with minimal
enthusiasm. Jezza is acceptably attractive. His six pack and
pecs protrude in an athletic fashion yet don't mask the dull
look in his eyes.

'You guys wouldn't happen to have a stubby holder?'
Danielle asks. 'This is going to boil in an instant otherwise.'

Derek rifles through his Esky and deck chair.

'Nah, sorry mate. They're back in the car. They've probably melted by now, anyway, so it'd be more useless than tits
on a bull.'

'We'll just have to drink fast,' Jane says.

Jane rolls her tongue around the lip of the bottle and
downs half in one gulp.

'Mmm, I can drink to that,' Jezza says, downing the last
of his beer. 'Chuck us another one, would ya.'

Derek throws a XXXX over the girls. Jane squeals
with delight as ice and chilled water drips across her bare
stomach. Danielle shivers with each drop that splashes onto
her body. The sensation is short lived with the blasting of
the sun and the heat of her skin evaporating the water in an
immediate sizzle.

Danielle shudders with realisation of what Jane has gotten her into. The scent of Jezza's salt-washed body sweating cloys her. She sits upright and hoists the beer to her lips, gulping down heavily. Each pump of liquid cools her throat. She inhales the beer as if it were a life-nurturing fuel. Air sucks through the can with her last gulp. She drops the tin and exhales a yeast-filled burp.

'Danielle,' Jane hisses.

'Thanks guys. I really needed that,' Danielle says. 'Have you got another?'

'My kind of girl,' Jezza claims. 'We've got as many as you can drink.'

He cracks another beer and hands it to Danielle. She embraces the cold metal in her hand. After a deep exhale she lifts the can and downs the beer as quickly as her stomach will allow. The gush of cold fluid soothes her mind. Each drop of alcohol smooths out any concerns about the situation. The can gasps again the instant the beer is down Danielle's throat.

'Fuck me,' Jezza exclaims.

'It's been a long morning. I needed it,' Danielle shrugs. 'Keep up, slow poke,' she says, smiling down at Jane.

'There's no way I'm being shown up by my little cuz,' Jane answers. She sits up and pours the Breezer down her throat. Her gag reflex kicks in and rejects the sudden rush of booze with a sharp sudden cough. Jane chokes it down. The bottle raises again for the piss to pour out. With a sigh of relief

Jane finishes the bottle. Another Breezer appears in Derek's hand the moment the first one is finished. Jane stares down her competition.

'C'mon. Don't be soft,' Danielle jibes with a sudden wave of drunken pleasure.

'I'll get all of this down,' Jane says, 'it might just take me a bit longer.'

She turns the bottle bottom up and empties it in a series of forced gulps. Short breaths struggle out between each gulp. Danielle sips gently on the coolness of a new beer, watching and smiling.

TELEVISIONS! FRIDGES! WASHERS! DRIERS! ALL AT LOW LOW LOW PRICES! BARTER TOWN HAS EVERY-THING YOU NEED FOR YOUR HOME. OUR HOMEWARE RANGE IS MASSIVE WITH BARGAINS TO MATCH. DON'T LIKE THE PRICE, THEN HAGGLE! WE LOVE CHATTING TO OUR CUSTOMERS TO MAKE SURE YOU GET THE BEST POSSIBLE PRICE. COME IN STORE TODAY. NOW IN TEN LOCATIONS.

Claire

Claire throws a judgemental glare at Tony and David as they whisper and sneak into the adjoining room. Tony's hand rests comfortably on David's back as he directs him from the room.

'The bestiality conversation must have got those two in the mood,' Claire murmurs to Simon while holding her fingers to her mouth as if smoking.

'What conversation?' Other Sam jumps in hearing their whispers.

'Matt was educating us about the intricacies of bestiality and necrophilia?' Sam explains, somehow proudly.

'Yep, that's the one I was talking about,' Claire speaks to the table. 'I still don't understand how a conversation like that comes about in the first place.'

'Oh, we've had many strange conversations over dinner,' Simon says. 'It's a good judge of character. You can see who's put off easily and who's pragmatic. We like to get into—let's say interesting—debates.'

Claire takes a swig of her Bolly.

'What a strange tradition,' Claire says.

'Who's strange?' Thomas jumps in. 'Tony? We knew that already. Wait, where is Tony?'

'They're off huffing away,' Claire points toward the door Tony and David disappeared behind.

'A joint, hey?' Thomas's eyes light up. 'From the usual guy?' he asks of Simon.

'Probably,' Simon shrugs.

'Excuse me, then.' Thomas dabs his lips on his napkin and slides out from the table. In three precise steps he ducks out of sight to follow Tony and David into the other room. A stench of weed smoke escapes through the door as it eases shut behind him.

'Good thing I bought extra beef jerky when I was shopping,' Simon says. 'Tony goes nuts for it whenever he's in the funny papers.'

'Funny papers?' Claire's eyebrow rises at her uncle.

'Yeah, funny papers. I can't be that old. Surely you know what that means.'

'Yes I do, but I haven't heard that in ages. I thought only people in movies called it that.'

'They have to get it from somewhere, or make it up, I suppose,' Simon says while standing. 'You guys can help me move all of this to the kitchen. I'll throw it in the dishwasher later but if it's in the kitchen it saves me a lot of work.'

Claire, Simon, Sam, Other Sam, Michael and Matt pile their plates and shuffle it all off into the kitchen. Their glasses and fresh bottles of wine wait at the table for their return.

'I should buy them smoking jackets,' Simon mutters as he walks past the room hiding the weed fanciers.

The group settle back down at the table. Matt pops open

a fresh bottle of Bollinger and places it next to an icy bottle of vodka.

'Hey hey,' he says, presenting the two bottles.

'Oh my. Yes please,' Michael shoves his glass across the table.

They all quickly jump at the sight of the chilled booze. Matt pours out half and half's of vodka and Bollinger and passes them down the table. Claire sniffs at the glass. The sting of alcohol floods her nostrils.

'By god that's good,' Simon announces after his first sip.

Claire takes a sip. A sudden divine numbness floats through her mind. The bubbles tingle like sherbet on her lips and the freezing vodka cools in a soothing delight down her throat.

'Oh my,' she exclaims after her first sip. 'Where do you get the idea for something like that?'

'I would say I learnt it growing up, which is kinda true,' Matt says.

'Yeah, watching Ab Fab,' Michael jokes.

'Long live Patsy,' Simon announces, throwing his glass up in the air.

'Long live Patsy,' the gays follow their host's lead, clinking their glasses together.

'Long live—um—Patsy,' Claire toasts.

They all down their glasses in time for the trio in the other room to re-emerge. Claire spots a ringed redness to David's eyes and a glow in his dumb smile.

'Good stuff then?' Matt asks.

'Um—um—yes,' Tony responds. His finger floats in the air as he struggles to process a thought.

'The jerky's in the fridge,' Simon cuts in.

Tony's face lights up. His finger curls back down, his thoughts answered. In a slow motion display of movement he walks pointedly from the room and into the kitchen. David meanders back over to his seat next to Claire, the pungent odour following him as he sits.

'What have you guys been doing?' he asks, sliding a hand deep between Claire's thighs.

'You know, the usual Australia Day tradition. Drinking,' Claire responds. She pulls his hand out, ignoring the tingles that run up her leg at his touch.

'Oh my god!' David exclaims. Everyone snaps their looks around to him for an answer. 'I could drink. Margaritas!' he declares.

'Margaritas!' the room shouts with enthusiasm.

'Shit yeah,' Simon says. 'To the tequila.'

In mere moments Simon has the blender loaded with tequila, cointreau, ice and lemon juice. The buzzing hums triggers anticipation building in the dining room that settles into a hush of expectation. The mechanical hum falls silent, and moments later Tony waltzes into the room with a silver tray full of cocktail glasses. The excess salt rimming the glasses sprinkles off with each step he takes.

'Margaritas!' he sings. 'Ma—Ma—Margaritas.'

Claire and David take theirs. David, in a delayed motion clinks his glass against the edge of Claire's. Claire lifts the glass to her lips and savours the taste of the salt. The tequila fumes burn in her nose. A quiver runs down her spine.

'Cheers,' she says.

'Cheers,' everyone echoes, raising their glasses.

A smug, slow grin forms on David's face as the weed powers the steam wheels churning in his head. Claire sips at the slushy drink. The fire of the excess tequila heats her throat. A rasping cough rises and chokes in her chest. On the other side of the table Thomas splutters out a stream of ice and booze. The table erupts in laughter.

IT'S THAT TIME OF YEAR, BACK TO SCHOOL TIME. ARE YOU READY? ALL YOUR BACK TO SCHOOL NEEDS ARE IN ONE LOCATION WITH BOOKS R US. BOOKS, PENS, BACKPACKS, EVERYTHING YOU NEED TO GET YOUR KIDS BACK TO SCHOOL. VISIT US ONLINE TO FIND OUT ABOUT OUR SPECIAL COLLECTION SERVICES. YOU SUBMIT YOUR CLASSES AND REQUIREMENTS ON OUR SIMPLE BOOKS R US ONLINE FORM AND WE DO THE REST. SIMPLY DROP IN AND COLLECT YOUR COMPLETE PRE-PACKAGED SCHOOL SUPPLIES. AT BOOKS R US WE MAKE BACK TO SCHOOL TIME A BREEZE.

'Oh, I forgot to mention,' Tony says. 'I may have slipped three or four times with the tequila. I just love it so much,' his voice trails off.

'I think I just came, this is so awesome,' David laughs, lowering the margarita glass.

'David!' Claire hisses and slaps him on the leg.

'Oh honey, if you were alone in a room with Tony we know you just came,' Other Sam quips.

'You're such a bitch,' Sam says, lowering his own glass. 'Blow me this is good, Tony.'

'You had your chance,' Tony sasses back.

'What's with tequila and making you guys so horny,' Simon says from the head of the table. 'I know it's all so tasty, but come on guys.'

'We usually do,' Thomas chuckles.

'Um wow,' Claire says. She pushes her chair back and stands for an announcement. 'So this escalated quickly. I'm gonna go out for a dip.' She hoists her glass up and downs the remainder of her margarita. She squints her eyes as her hand smacks into her head.

'Ha, brain freeze,' Thomas points out.

'Yep,' Claire seethes. 'Are you coming for a dip, David? The water is probably lovely at the moment.'

David stares intently at the condensation building and dripping down the side of his glass.

'David,' Claire repeats.

'Huh? What, yeah sure,' he answers.

'Cool lets go. I may be wanting another margarita, Tony, once you guys have cooled off,' Claire says.

She tugs on David's hand and leads him out the door. The trek down to the beach runs via the car park rather than through the dunes. The crowd on the beach sizzles under the sun. The red masses of lobster-skinned people begin to cluster under the little shade available on the beach. David reaches into Claire's bikini and pinches at her nipple.

'Ow,' Claire slaps at his hand. A tingling numbness runs from her nipple and across her chest. She bites her lip, noticing the lack of attention from the crowds covering the beach. 'Wait until we get into the water, I suppose,' Claire states openly.

David's face twinkles with sudden eager delight. Claire grips harder onto his wrist and drags him through the crowd. They pass a couple of girls laughing flirtatiously under the attentions of a pair of blokes either side of them, who are staring directly at the girls' boobs. The beach clears slightly as they walk further away from the town. Claire slides off her shirt and boardies. David drops his shirt on the ground in the same pile and the pair wade out to the chest-deep waves of the ocean.

'The sand feels insane right now,' David says.

'How's your footing?' Claire asks. 'Not too rough out here for you?'

'Good enough, I reckon I'm floating well. Why?'

Claire's legs wrap around David's waist. She grinds her bikini covered snatch against David's crotch.

'Because I have an idea,' she says. No one's attention is drawn to the affectionate couple in the water. 'Let's move with the waves.'

'Um, what?' David asks, confused.

Claire pulls on the velcro of David's boardies. She rips the fly open and eases her hand in onto his penis. His cock swells the instant her hand touches its flesh. She pulls it out and jerks it until he is fully stiff in the palm of her hand.

'Oh, I see now,' David gloats.

'Oh do you now?'

Claire slides her bikini to one side and shoves David's dick inside her with a sigh of pleasure.

'Let's take as long as it needs,' she yelps at the rush of adrenaline through her body.

Claire glances around. No one has paid any interest to them. *We must look like any couple on the beach*, Claire thinks to herself as she slides back and forth on David's poised cock.

@DerekRussell #AustraliaDay rocks. Totes chucking a sickie tomoz.

Recess: O'philia, o'philia: A grandly short ode to the men with the sort of goods you desire

Her hand grips onto the rock hard body. It is cool to the touch, still not warmed from the crackling fire they lay before. She presses her back against the silky smooth fur of the rug. A drop of sweet moisture drips down her chin and onto her collarbone. It's an instant cool tickle on her skin. The moment it touches her skin the drop sizzles with the same excitement running through her body. It isn't her first threesome, and definitely won't be her last, yet the same thrill and chills run through her in anticipation of what's to come.

She loosens her blouse to allow her breasts to heave lusciously. Ben and his friend continue to work their magic on her. Her tongue continues to devour the sweet taste coming from them. An occasional bitter hint seeps through her mouth. Her mind recalls these delightful flavours. She's been here before.

A harder crackle fires out of the flames as the weight

of the top log crushes the coals. A spark flickers out of the fireplace and hisses as it touches her skin. A sigh of pain and pleasure intertwining peaks inside her. A sudden rush of blood pumps through her veins. Her heart pulses with the ecstasy. She knows what's coming. It will be the first of many. Her toes curl. A moan rises from her throat as the pressure in her head builds into a full brain freeze. That's the risk you take eating ice cream unprotected.

PART IV

Cassandra

'Good evening, I'm Cassandra Cummings with your 5CCB evening news update. Fire has broken out on the outskirts of Founders Bay. A CFS spokesperson has confirmed it's a small, slow-travelling blaze moving in a thin band through the nature reserve and is currently contained. CFS volunteers are on standby to monitor the situation and extinguish any flare-ups. Police and fire authorities warn people to be watchful for any fires and remind travellers to never drive into smoke even if you think you know your way on the roads.

'In other news, the temperature reached its maximum of forty-three point three degrees at four o'clock today. The Bureau of Meteorology forecasts that the temperature will hold through most of the evening with only small decreases through what will be a sweltering night.

'Reports of racial vilification have risen from the Survival Day commemorative event at the Founders Bay town square. The reports say that a group of passing tourists yelled racial taunts and threw food at the event's participants. Event organiser Aunty May Johnson said it was a minor incident and it would not ruin the significance of the day.

'In sport, Dwayne Story has taken out the Coonawarren Australian of the Year for his commitment to sport and his representation of the country in the international sporting arena. John Carclew took out the Coonawarren Senior Citizen of the Year for his thirty years of volunteer work at his residential retirement home and Ladasher Simms was awarded Young Citizen of the Year for the page she created on Facebook promoting the youth events around the district.

'Very warm and thirty-eight tonight with a top of forty-five predicted tomorrow. I'm Cassandra Cummings. I'll return in an hour with your next 5CCB news update.'

Simon

Tony moves his seat closer to Simon's, sliding his margarita glass across with him.

'So,' he whispers. 'Where do you think those two ducked off to in such a hurry?'

'Well,' Simon answers. He clasps his hands together and bats his eyelids daintily. 'I'm betting they ducked off for a sneaky root, just like last year.'

'Didn't they do that this morning?' Sam chimes from the other end of the table. 'And you guys should learn to whisper more quietly.'

The men at the table stop their own conversations, chairs scraping on the cement as they lean forward. The only sounds are hushed sips on the edge of their margarita glasses as they wait for Simon to continue.

'Tony,' Simon warns.

'What?' Tony shrugs. 'It's not like they were quiet about it. Well not David anyway.'

'A bit of a grunter is he? Snorting pig after truffles?' Thomas laughs. The guests erupt in hysterics but quickly shush the moment Simon clears his throat.

'Yeah, he may be, a little bit,' Simon says.

'Not just a bit. Even from outside I could hear the groans,' Tony jokes. 'It didn't go for long though. I imagine her saying "well done" or "good for you" once he cums.' Other Sam claps through the fresh crackle of laughter. His slapping hands pierce the air and the ears of Sam sitting next to him.

'Ouch,' Sam complains. 'Between that and your sneezing I'm gunna have to send you the bill for my ENT doctor.'

'Suck it up, princess,' Other Sam dismisses.

'That's queen to you,' Sam snaps back.

'Anyway you two,' Simon cuts back in. 'They did the exact same thing last year. Tony took him out the back to get high, then they disappeared for a shag. Claire says it's hard to find the space and time together while she's sharing a tiny unit.'

'I bet it's hard,' Tony laughs.

'Probably not now,' Thomas says slyly.

Tony slides closer again to Simon. He purrs as he strokes his chin against Simon's shoulder.

'All this talk of young passion makes me want to cool off,' he says.

Simon looks down into Tony's batting eyelids. A glint of pleasure shimmers across his features.

'I suppose we could go for a dip in our usual spot,' Simon says, stroking the back of his hand down Tony's cheek and chin.

'Yay,' Tony jumps out of his seat. He throws the half-full glass of margarita down his throat and shakes out the zing of tequila in his mouth. 'I'll grab the towels. Who else is coming?'

'Coming where?' Sam asks.

'Just down to a nice stretch of beach we know. The tourists avoid it because it's too far away from the town's conveniences,' Simon states.

'Oh cool,' Sam says.

'I don't have anything to wear,' Other Sam adds.

'You don't need to worry about that,' Tony says. 'I won't be wearing anything once we hit the water either.'

'What? Seriously? It's not even a nude beach,' Other Sam says.

'So?' Tony questions. 'No one else goes there.'

'Fuck it, I'm in,' Other Sam stands up. 'You've all seen it all before anyway.'

The other men quickly down their drinks. Thomas sneaks an extra glass of Veuve and snorts through the sudden rush of bubbles tingling his nose. They fall into file behind Simon as they set their empty glasses at the end of the table before they tread out onto the burning sand. Tony follows the group juggling a pile of mismatched towels, the hideous greens and yellows of the faded cotton bounce as Tony steps out into the sun and onto the uneven dunes.

EAST AUSTRALIA UNIVERSITY OFFERS THE GREATEST RANGE OF SCIENCE DEGREES OF ALL THE AUSTRALIAN UNIVERSITIES. OUR PROFESSIONAL TEAM OF LECTURERS AND STATE OF THE ART RESEARCH FACILITIES ARE WHAT MAKE GROUNDBREAKING DISCOVERIES HAPPEN. EAU IS ALWAYS ON THE SEARCH FOR AUSTRALIA'S NEWEST AND BRIGHTEST MINDS. HAVE YOU GOT WHAT IT TAKES TO JOIN AUSTRALIA'S PREMIERE SCIENCE UNIVERSITY? ENROL NOW OR CONTACT OUR HELPFUL ADMIN TEAM FOR MORE INFORMATION.

Danielle and Jane scull the tasteless beer. Jezza and Derek sit across from them chanting in awe at the girls' ability to gulp booze so quickly. The girls throw the empties into the sand with a powdered smack.

'Whoa, you girls sure know how to have a good time,' Jezza says. He takes a steady sip on his stubby.

'Yeah, I can't believe we didn't catch up with you girls last year. It woulda been awesome drinking like that with you guys then as well,' Derek adds.

'Well,' Danielle begins. She pauses and holds up a drunken finger for silence. A pale flash floods across her face. A heave rises from her stomach. Jane leans away from her cousin ready to dodge the projectile vomit. Danielle gasps and releases a foul burp in the direction of the water. She breathes back in, colour flushing back to her cheeks. 'Well, you guys would be more fun if you kept up.'

'Dani,' Jane hisses, 'that was disgusting.'

'That was awesome,' Jezza and Derek say in admiration.

Jane frowns at the two blokes, but her glares go unnoticed as they focus their enthusiasm on Danielle's every move. They ignore Jane's attempts at flirting, not even responding when she let her boob slide out her bikini top. Somehow Danielle's mannish ways has scored her more male attention and free drinks than she'd seen any bimbo act achieve before.

The guys dive into the Esky in a mad scramble to grab the next beer. They slap at each other's hands, splashing icy water out onto Jane. She cringes silently as the blokes play out their sudden eagerness. Jezza and Derek straighten from the Esky and each hold out a bottle for Danielle.

'Cheers,' she says, taking both.

'Excuse me,' Jane bats her eyelids up at Derek. 'May I have one as well?'

'Sure, they're in the Esky,' he answers back.

Jane exhales above the crashing sound of the waves. She reaches into the Esky and pulls out a can of XXXX. *May as well keep up*, she thinks to herself, swallowing half the beer in the first drink.

'So Dani, what team do you root for?' Jezza asks.

'Is that a trick question?' Danielle replies.

'I go for Essendon,' Jane states. The boys ignore her.

'Well only if you don't barrack for the Giants,' Derek says.

'What if I don't barrack for any team? I'd rather watch the netball instead,' Danielle says.

'You're a netball chick,' Derek exclaims. 'I love those full body skirt things they wear.'

Danielle laughs in response. She cracks open the first beer and returns to drinking rather than conversing with the boys.

'Your folks don't care that you're down here drinking?' Jezza asks.

'Meh, I don't think they notice,' Danielle shrugs. 'All they care about is us having sunscreen on. We'll just do the same as every other time, tell them we don't feel well and stay in our rooms until we're sober.'

Derek slides his hand onto Danielle's leg. She keeps drinking, barely registering the sudden warmth of his sweaty palm through the tingly numbness from the booze. The rough grip of his fingers is masked by the layer of alcoholic plaster running in her system.

'So, you have your own room here?' Derek whispers.

'Yeah but it's guarded. Don't you guys have a place?' Danielle answers.

'Not really. We'll just crash wherever and head home again tomorrow morning.'

'Although, we could sneak into the house,' Jezza suggests. 'It looks like most of our crew are on the beach or already passed out up in the shade.'

'May as well,' Danielle shrugs. 'Bring the Esky and some music. You guys got an iPhone?'

Danielle sprays sand across the towel as she stands up and smacks her back and arse.

'I think I need a few more before we do this,' Jane whispers close to Danielle.

'What for? I thought you fucked guys all the time?'

'Well, kinda. I usually wait for the buzz to kick in first. You're doing great, getting heaps of drinks out of those suckers.'

Jane cranes her neck to peer over the dunes at the trio of houses. She can't spot her aunt and uncle but the rest of the family can be seen staring intensely at the palms of their hands. *Boring,* she thinks, *they're playing cards already.* She looks further down the beach. People crowd the beach near the car park entrance and houses, a layer of red bodies lie with drinks buried in the sand next to them. A couple of people sit waist deep in the water, grins of relief on their faces. Further down the sand a group of men dash into the water. Jane squints through the sandy haze. The last set of white arse cheeks dashes to the water as the men streak across the beach. *Well he's going to have some drag*, she thinks, spotting the shadow of a swinging cock between his legs.

Grant

'You know I don't want to do this,' Grant whispers. His pet murmurs in response. 'What's that?'

A black mass slinks out of the shadows. The dark latex zentai stretches across the floor in a short, skinny mound of a human body. A chain from his neck tinkles lightly across the cold cement floor. A muffled response sounds out from behind the zip across the gimp's face.

'Oh, hold on, let me fix that for you,' Grant offers. He holds the back of his head in his hand and eases the metal zip open. 'There you go.'

The pet sucks in a waft of fresh air before lifting himself up to sit cross-legged next to Grant. He hunches at his neck as he talks down to the cement.

'I know you don't want to do it,' the pet says in a soft, croaking voice. Under his lip harsh scruff pops out from behind the zip. 'But it's come to that time. I knew to expect this when I started.'

Grant reaches to the pet's chin and pulls his eyes up to meet his. The pet's grey eyes stare calmly back.

'I have never wanted to let you go,' Grant tears up. 'We've had you for years. You've been perfect for us. I don't want to give any of that up.'

'You were perfect for me too and you don't have to give up any of those moments we had together. You'll remember those forever. Like the time the Mistress smacked you and made you repeat every blow with me until we all came five times that night. You were so good the bruise on my cheek lasted weeks.'

'There were some good times,' Grant reminisces. His eyes open with a newfound wonder. 'I always pondered what it would be like if I was the master for a night and Helen the sub.'

'Is it too wrong of me to ask if you ever did have control?' The pet shrinks away the moment his question sneaks out.

'There's no need to shy away. I only do what people ask of me. I was allowed to be in charge when Helen let me. It's how we had the kids. But since then she has always been in control and I've done what she wanted. Well, all except get rid of you before now.'

'You did try though, I was with you when you wrote those ads for the Trading Post and Gumtree,' the pet encourages. 'They were very well written. I'm just getting old. No one wants an old gimp and you can't give me away. We all know what has to happen now.'

'I know,' Grant says, gripping tentatively at the hacksaw's handle. 'But losing you means finding a replacement. I don't think I have the heart for it anymore.'

'You had others before me, what happened to those?' A hint of rising confidence shows in his voice.

'We re-homed them. Last I heard the Sampsons still have one of them. They're really happy with how it worked out.'

'Just like how we are all really happy with how things have been,' he smiles through the latex mask. 'I have loved my time with you. You were my first and only masters and I couldn't have asked for better.'

A tear forms in the corner of Grant's eyes. His cheeks flush red and his chin quivers at such sweet eyes and words.

'You've been the best friend a man could ever have,' he whimpers.

'And you've been the best owner a slave could have,' the pet answers.

They slump into a heaving embrace. The stench of sweat-filled latex floods Grant's mind with beautiful memories.

The rawness of his pet's skin runs like roughly dried cotton under his fingers. The foulness of the unbrushed teeth shoots memories of passionate embraces and smacks titillate Grant's spine.

'It's time to let me go,' the sub continues. Grant nods. 'But can I beg a final favour?'

'Anything,' Grant wipes his eyes on his collar. 'You can have anything you want before it happens.'

'Can we have one final special moment together?' Grant's teeth grin through his lips at the thought. 'But this time, can you be Helen as well as yourself?'

'What? How do you mean?'

'I want to just be with you, but I want you to strike with Helen's malice. Channel her to strike the final blow. It would be perfect for me.'

Grant nods. He leans in for a final sickly sweet embrace. His soft lips scratch against the beard around his pet's lips. His pet offers his tongue in return, tracing the shape of Grant's smooth teeth and lips in one last grasp at memories. The man and his pet separate. Grant stands over him, a straightening force of strength fills his spine.

'Are you ready?' Grant asks. The pet nods.

'Be as fierce as Helen, but keep the care in your eyes. Don't stop until I'm gone.'

Keith

The moment Keith hoists on and buckles his CFS overalls he starts sweating heavily into the thick fabric. The thrashing of the hot wind through the truck window does nothing to cool the sweltering heat against his skin. The siren and lights blare from the roof above them. In the short distance a long plume of smoke blows a black mark into the sky in a line the length of the town. With few members of the public sober enough to drive the road is completely clear for their charge in to work.

Keith shoves a finger into his overalls and yanks at the collar. A large dollop of sweat gushes down his neck, sliding straight to his chest under the singlet.

140

'Thank god it's just the one fire,' Keith mutters. 'Then I can be done with uniforms for the day.'

He lifts up his map to look closer at the property they are charging towards. The paper flaps against Keith's knuckles as he tries to read the fence lines.

'Looks like the Clayton's southern gate is going to be the easiest to get into,' he shouts to the driver.

'Will we be able to get into the scrub from there?' Nathaniel, the short Filipino, yells back.

'Yes, should be right. Their back paddock sits on the national park line. Clayo won't mind if we break in and use some of his sand as a containment line. Knowing him I reckon he'll have the front end loader out there already.'

The road bends steadily as the truck eases to a smoother speed so that the crew's eyes can seek out the entrance to the property. The smoke blows directly overhead from their new facing.

'There it is,' Cameron, Nathaniel's brother, says from the front.

To the left of the truck a short rubble track runs over to a wide steel gate. Keith jumps down from the cab. He jogs as roughly as he can past the growling engine to unlatch the gate. Keith looks out across the flat paddock as the truck cranks past him. His prediction is right. Clayo is standing next to his front end loader, a long line of sand scraped up to the back fence of his property. Nearby his son stands on the back of a ute, a large tank of water and hydraulic pump on the back.

'About time,' Clayo yells to Keith as the truck arrives. 'I called you guys well over an hour ago.'

'Well you know us, fashionably late,' Keith jokes. He throws his hand out on approach to Clayo. The rough farmers' hands clench together in a matey embrace. 'The operator said it was a long one. Looks like you've gone all out with the containment line.'

'Yeah mate, all precautions. Most of this we put out at the start of the season. Luckily, the fire doesn't look too wide. Long, skinny bastard following the tree line. Neville's by the ute with one tank and I've got the extinguisher ready to take out any embers that jump over. We should be right now you're here.'

Keith sighs and looks back toward the source of the fire. The flames aren't far off now. Heat radiates out from the scrub in front of them.

'Just gonna have to let it burn,' Keith confirms his previous thoughts to the other volunteers. 'The scrub is too thick. No way to get in safely. We can take out the edge of the blaze once it hits here. We'll have to wait for the planes to be done with the fires further up north, they're apparently threatening homes already. Hopefully no one's stupid enough to be camping in the scrub here today.'

'So mate, how's things back in town?' Clayo starts the banter.

'It's been a busy hot one today. The town's packed again.'

'I'm sure you've been keeping busy, Mr Mayor,' Clayo slaps Keith on the back. 'How's your place? All packed up safely?'

'Yeah, as well as can be. The sheep are huddling in the shade of a windbreak, well away from the back scrub. They've got the big block so should be right.'

'Should be right for you, you're not on the main road where heaps of dickheads just flick their butts out the window.'

An intense blast of heat snaps Clayo and Keith away from their banter.

'Back to it then,' Keith says.

Keith climbs onto the back of the truck to man the main hose. Two other volunteers jump up with him and grip onto the driver's side hose. A fresh stink of burnt wood blows out from the scrub. An insidious crackling edges closer to the property. The volunteers and owners prepare to drive back and forth, drowning the flames and any spark that skips over the containment line.

Jacko and Jonno

Jonno shoves Jacko hard in the chest. Jacko stumbles back onto the couch, yanking his fly shut as he does.

'What the fuck was that dude?' Jonno shouts at him, he shoves again.

'What the fuck was what man?' Jacko pushes back.

'That wasn't right. I'm not a fucking faggot dude. It's fucking wrong what they do. I don't want no queer cunt homo bastard thinking I'm one of them. What the hell happened?'

The manic rush washes over them. Jacko's eyes dart wildly around the room. Burning sparks stab throughout his body. The twitching remnants of his orgasm continues to spasm in his limbs. Jacko slides into the kitchen to pace the tiles, his feet barely skimming the floor with the speed in his steps. Jonno walks up behind Jacko and stares fiercely down at him. His face flushes with a haze of rage. Jacko catches the hatred in his eyes.

'I know what it was,' Jacko's lips twitch out. 'It was those fuckin' muzzos. It's them and their ways. They don't want to accept our lifestyle so they force their own weird shit onto us.'

Mark

Mark snaps out of his daze when the frantic footsteps of his manager stomp past him. He arches up from the bottom potato chip shelf to follow the action as the manager marches to the front of the shop, whispering hectically into the phone pressed against his ear. Mark eases up from the floor. The greasy smell of fatty burgers floats down the aisles from the free takeaway stand at the front of the store.

'I know. I can't believe it,' Mark hears his manager whisper as he approaches the main entrance. 'This has gone too far. I think we are going fine without cutting anymore. Our tills were at record numbers when I checked at lunch. What? Um? Are you sure, sir? Yes, okay. I will sort something out. All of it? What sir? One dollar? Yes, fine. Whatever you say.'

His manager hangs up the phone, shaking his head.

'I can't believe it,' he says to Mark. 'Look at those bastards in Cottonvalue. They cut everything in half. Nothing is over half price plus they're giving away all that food out front.'

'Just like we are?' Mark nods toward the families lining up for the free feed.

'Yes. But now we're dropping the price of everything in store to one dollar.'

'What? Why the hell would we do that?'

'Because we're told to. It's an "Australia Day clearance". It's up on social media already. Everything has to go today. They've already shipped the next load of stock from the warehouse for us so they want everything in here gone before the trucks arrive.'

'Damn it,' Mark's shoulders drop. 'We won't be able to leave until it's all shelved again, will we?'

'Nope. Even if it means sleeping the night here—what the fuck—' the manager's voice trails off. 'That bastard.'

Mark looks out to the plaza courtyard. He shakes his head in disbelief. Cottonvalue's manager is handing out trays of meat and soft drinks to the shoppers in the plaza. Each distributed gift steps him closer and closer to the main entrance of Ash's. Before Mark can latch onto his manager's arm he's already charging through the main door.

The automatic doors slide elegantly out of the way for Mark's manager to charge out at his competition. Mark dashes after his manager with a sudden burst of adrenaline.

'Excuse me ma'am,' Mark's manager says in a sickly sweet manner to the lady receiving a tray of barbecue sausages. 'Could I please steal this gentleman away from you for a moment?'

'Certainly, sweetie,' the elderly lady says, hobbling toward the shopping centre entrance.

The managers stand up straight, puffing their chests at each other. Their crisply pressed shirts bulge symmetrically down their bodies. The mirrored badges, phones and pens sit straight in position. Mark smirks, amused by the pair of managers fronting up. He remarks to himself that if it weren't for the colours and logos he wouldn't be able to tell the managers apart.

'May I ask what you are doing this close to our supermarket handing out your produce?' Mark's manager seethes.

'I am simply sharing the spirit of Australia Day with all the shopping centre's customers. I assume you are doing the same,' Cottonvalue's manager responds arrogantly.

'I believe everyone should be enjoying the spirit of Australia Day but you are in violation of our lease agreement. This area belongs to us.'

Their chests rise even further, fit to burst.

'You can't tell me where I can and cannot stand around here. I have permission from Head Office to hand out produce wherever I like. And once they taste how good our produce is then your customers will become our regulars.'

'Liar,' Mark's manager shoves the palm of his hand into his rival's chest.

A look of shock mingles with boiling rage on his rival's face. The man shoves back. The pair trade blows back and forth. Mark stands back, refusing to dirty his hands in the rivalry. He watches on along with the confused costumers who gather around the scene.

Mark's manager smacks a meat tray to the floor. The raw steaks slap on the ground. The wrestling limbs and crinkling uniforms tumble to the ground too. They toss and roll on each other, shoving with their hands and knees.

WANT TO ESCAPE THE HEAT? TRAVEL CENTRE HAS EXCLUSIVE NEW ZEALAND HOLIDAY PACKAGES AT INCREDIBLE PRICES. OUR SELECTION OF TRAVEL CENTRE PACKAGES HAS SOMETHING FOR EVERYONE, FROM FAMILIES TO COUPLES AND EVERYTHING

Simon

'So how do we do this?' Other Sam asks.

The group of men stand around a pile of folded towels lying on the sand where Tony had dropped them. No one else is within half a kilometre of the men. Other Sam squints as he tries to make out the faces of the closest group of people, but he can't see anything from this distance. The only visible detail is a bright pink bikini. Behind them thick scrub saddles a rocky plain to the edge of the sand and rides it back as far as he can see. A line of smoke rises from the distance. He shrugs it off—bushfires are just part of the Australian way of life in summer, it's no big deal. Other Sam has a more pressing dilemma in front of him. He looks back to the circle of feet on the sand, not yet ready to lift his gaze higher. The warm buzz of the Bolly helps though. Other Sam can feel a rising flamboyance and he can see it also building in his friends.

'Well this is how it's done,' Tony declares.

Tony grabs the hem of his shirt, rips it off and dumps

148

it on the towels. He yanks his pants down to expose his completely tanned body and the pants follow the shirt onto the pile. He twists and dashes to the water, leaving the group in his wake. The water splashes out with each mad kick as he runs into the shallows, then swallows him as he flops into the water.

The friends look back at each other. The walk to the beach has layered every part of their bodies with sweat. The late sun sears their skin, even piercing through their clothes. They trade nervous glances, then shrug away their reservations. They slip out of their clothes and throw them onto the growing pile of fabric on the sand. The Aussiebum jocks and ES briefs flop on top of the pile.

A stampede of feet kicks up a storm of sand as several self-conscious men scramble for the coverage of the water. They giggle like guilty teens as they flop about far enough into the shallows to cover their junk.

'I didn't realise how much of an otter you are, Matt,' Sam says once they're backstroking themselves deeper against the waves.

'Seriously? I'm totally a surprise otter,' Matt says, flopping his hair back into the warm water. 'You think I'm all straight and narrow and then I take my shirt off and bam! Otter!'

'This is fantastic Simon. You guys must be out here all the time.' Matt says.

'Yeah, most nights in summer,' Simon replies. Tony

nuzzles up against his partner while Simon talks. 'Usually we don't have to walk so far out though,' he continues over the nibbling on his ears. 'Australia Day fills up the beach though so we have to move further up.'

'Ouch! What the fuck was that!' Sam shrieks. 'Who the fuck did that? That's not funny. It hurt!'

Sam splashes at his leg in the water. He gasps for air through the salt water washing over his face.

'What's all that for?' Tony shouts over the splashing.

'It fucking hurts! That's what it's for!' Sam cries.

'Come off it. It's probably just some seaweed or a pissed off crab because you stepped on his head,' Other Sam remarks.

'Wouldn't be the first time he's had trouble with crabs,' Michael smirks. He splashes a blast of water at Sam with the palm of his hand.

'Fuck off guys. It fucking hurt,' Sam continues to shriek. 'It feels like I've been stung.'

'You better hope it wasn't a box jellyfish,' Michael teases. He wiggles his fingers up and down in a taunting flicker.

'Don't be stupid, Michael,' Tony answers. 'We don't get the box ones out here. Maybe a bluebottle but nothing more than that.'

Sam relaxes a bit at Tony's reassurance. The pain is still excruciating, but he feels a little better.

'Um,' Simon leans into Tony's ear. 'We do sometimes get box jellyfish here. We're in a bay and right next to the creek mouth. We've never worried about them much because they don't move far unless there's a storm, but they are here.'

'What! There's box jellyfish here?!' Tony exclaims.

'I was talking softly,' Simon whispers. 'To not panic Sam and cause his heart rate to escalate.'

'Oh shit,' Tony gasps. 'We should maybe swim away?'

'Slowly,' Simon instructs, leading the drunken paddle away from where they were floating.

'I've been stung by a box jellyfish?' Sam gasps.

'We don't know that,' Other Sam comforts him. 'It may have just been a bluebottle.'

'Just a bluebottle,' Sam exclaims in disbelief. 'Just a fucking bluebottle. Someone piss on my leg because it fucking stings.'

The group cringe at the thought.

'We're not all into watersports,' Matt states.

'I don't give a shit about watersports,' Sam gasps. 'Just someone piss on my leg it's really killing me.'

No one appears keen to volunteer.

'So who needs to pee the most?' Tony says.

'I'm feeling pretty keen to get out of the water. I guess I could piss on him too,' Michael offers.

'Good, you go pee on Sam's leg,' Tony directs.

Sam and Michael share a look. This won't be the weirdest thing they've ever done. They both shrug and begin the meander back to the shallows, Sam leaning on Michael as he struggles through the water. The remaining group watch

their naked bodies slowly emerge out of the water. The
tan lines of their briefs are soon clearly visible even at the
distance from the group.

Sam limps on his left leg as it becomes exposed to the
air. Sam stops at the shin deep water and holds his leg out
to Michael in a plea of mercy. Michael cringes at the angry
red welts stretching from Sam's knee down to the ankle. He
looks over Sam's head to the crowds along the stretch of the
beach, shouting and splashing about caught up in their own
worlds. No one looks to the far end of the beach where the
men swim free and nude. Only their friends are watching
them.

'Are you ready?' Michael asks. 'It's probably not as good
as fucking a dead guy, but it's better than nothing.'

'Just do it,' Sam glowers back, too desperate to defend
himself against the quip.

Michael shrugs again. The group watch him intently
as he pinches onto his shaft and aims it toward Sam's leg.
Sam squints away from Michael, waiting for the onslaught
of steaming liquid. Michael's chest heaves and drops in the
forced state of relaxation. A few quick exhales and hot piss
starts to stream smoothly out onto Sam's leg. Droplets spray
in a golden mist as it splashes onto Sam's leg.

Michael grins despite himself as the pulse of liquid from
his cock relieves the tension in his bladder. Sam stumbles
under the impact of the stream. He hobbles for a moment
as his balance fights unsuccessfully against the motion of

the waves. He splatters backwards into the shallow waves. Michael keeps pissing, unable to control it mid-stream. His piss goes wasted into the water.

The nude onlookers yell out in concern and start to rush over. Michael's stream slows to a dribble as he gapes open-mouthed at Sam's body twitching in the water. He releases his cock and snatches onto the back of Sam's head to hold his face above the waves. Michael's face turns white as it drains of blood, a look that is mirrored by his approaching friends.

Michael heaves at the back of Sam's head. Sam's neck rises limp out of the water, barely supported by the shakes of Michael's arms.

'What the fuck is happening? Did he just cum?' Tony tries to lift the mood. His twitching jaw barely manages to show any indication of humour.

Michael pushes his finger to Sam's throat.

Each blip of time slides into the next in slow motion. The naked men crowd around their supine friend in the ankle deep water, waiting to know what's happening.

Michael turns to look up into the ring of faces. He holds Sam's neck in his hands, the body limp in the surf.

'He's dead!' Michael screams.

Jane and Danielle

A blast of chilled air greets Danielle and Jane as they step inside their neighbour's beach house. They're greeted by angry shouts firing back and forth between two young men in the kitchen the moment the door opens.

'It's all their fault,' one of the guys shouts. 'I can believe this. We need to make sure this never happens again.'

The second guy stands eerily still except for the constant nodding. His head bops enthusiastically with each outburst from his mate. Their eyes meet in a wild stare that doesn't

154

snap back to reality when the door opens with a loud click.

'Um, we're just going to crash in here for a bit to cool off,' Derek says to the guys in the kitchen.

'They think they can just come in here and mess with everything we do. We need to get out there and make things change in this town,' the first guy continues. 'Those immigrants are the reason this all went to shit.'

'Phew,' Derek sighs. 'I think they're just high. We can sneak upstairs.'

The four of them stumble up the stairs. The carpet on the steps softly welcomes their heated feet. The pair in the kitchen don't flinch or glance up from their ranting as the group walks clumsily out of the room. They reach the second level hallway and try the doors they pass. The first few open to expose compact rooms loaded with as many bunk beds and built-in wardrobes as is possible, leaving a small floor space to walk in.

'How about this one?' Derek says from one of the doors.

A master bedroom sprawls before them. A few searing beams of sunlight circumvent the heavy curtains and lights the entire room in a shadowy yellow. A built-in wardrobe leads across the near wall to a door to the ensuite. A king-size bed coated in an oriental printed quilt fills the bulk of the room.

'This should do nicely,' Jezza says.

Jezza bounces into the room and across to the ensuite. He dumps his Esky in the middle of the bedroom in his hurry into the bathroom.

'I'll drink to that,' Danielle mumbles.

'You alright?' Jane says, her tongue slurs around her teeth as she talks.

'Yeah, just thirsty. That walk really took it out of me.'

Danielle stumbles over to the Esky and pulls out another stubby of XXXX each for her and Jane. They drop onto the bed in a sigh of comfort.

'Well, cheers to escaping Australia Day with my parents,' Danielle says. Jane clinks her bottle against Danielle's.

'Cheers to that,' Jane says. 'Your parents are weird.'

'True that.'

'True that?' Jane laughs and sways.

'They're messed up. The other week I heard them talking about pets but we've never had one. Well not since my goldfish died when I was ten.'

'What the hell? What were they talking about then?'

'Fuck knows, probably "the pet" is code for dad's cock.'

'Gross, as if you could even say something like that,' Jane stutters. 'I could never say that about my dad, just gross.'

'I'm too drunk to picture it, lol,' Danielle sways. She hoists the beer up and downs the remaining liquid in a couple of smooth gulps.

Jane squints at her cousin's XXXX. It empties seemingly without effort. Shame floats through her mind, unable to match the drinking skills of her cousin a month younger than her. Envy hazes her sight. She raises her own stubby and tips the beer down. The cold brew fizzes and gags in her throat. She splutters through it to swig the last of the beer.

The last beer fogs Jane's mind. The heaviness throws her off balance. A tinkle sounds in the room as she collapses onto the floor next to the bed along with her empty bottle.

A gripping cold wraps around Danielle. She sees splutters of light flicker through the drunken mist that hangs in front of her eyes.

'Girls, girls. You really need to check this out,' a faint voice drifts across her mind. 'You wanna check this out or—' it trails off.

A shiver crawls along the top of Danielle's skin. It runs along her stomach to her belly button. It settles into an intense itch. Danielle's fingers twitch, aching to reach out and scratch it. Her thoughts become flustered in the irritation deepened through her. Her arms flop exhausted next to her. Darkness washes in and out of her mind.

A beat thuds repetitively in the room around Danielle. The sound bumps her awake. A glimpse of Jezza and Derek standing over her passes momentarily into view. The blurred details of their bodies quickly dissipate into shadows.

Danielle's skin prickles. Warm breath rushes down the side of her neck. She fails to tense her muscles ready to jump away from the cold presence hovering near her. *What is that? Who's there?* she tries to whisper. A groan croaks from her mouth. What remains of her voice retreats inside her, hiding from the growing shadows around her. *It's just a dream. Nothing is here to get you*, Danielle tells herself. *Go back to sleep.*

The smell of fabric softener clamouring up Danielle's nose greets her as she emerges out of a daze. The fogginess continues to cloud her mind. Sleepiness controls her steady breathing into the quilt underneath her. The warmth of each breath blasts back up against her throat. Chilled sweat drips off her skin. She freezes at the sight of shadows lingering around her still. *It's just a dream*, she tries. The shadows don't listen. They hover around her, pressing close to her skin. An ache in her leg tingles.

Danielle squeezes her eyes shut. She uses the bed's rocking motion to drift into a blissful unconsciousness.

HAVE YOU SEEN SOMETHING SUSPICIOUS BUT DON'T KNOW WHAT TO DO? DID A FRIEND MENTION SOMETHING THAT FELT A LITTLE OFF? ARE THERE TOO MANY CARS VISITING A NEIGHBOUR'S HOUSE? DO YOU NOT FEEL SAFE? REPORT IT. CALL THE AUSTRALIAN GOVERNMENT TERRORISM HOTLINE ON 1800 TERROR. ANY SMALL SUSPICION OR FEAR CAN HELP US SAVE AUSTRALIAN LIVES. EVERY BIT OF INFORMATION HELPS.

'Fuck them. Those brown bastards up the road,' anger sparks in Jonno's eyes. 'It's their fault I was almost no longer a man. We gotta get 'em.'

'It's all their fault,' Jacko shouts. 'I can't believe this. We need to make sure it never happens again. This is our country. Fuck their queer shit.'

Jonno stands still and nods viciously. His head nods enthusiastically with each word from his mate. Their eyes meet each other's in a wild stare, they are together in this moment.

'They think they can just come over here and mess with our way of life. We need to get out there and make things change in this town,' Jacko continues. 'Those immigrants are to blame for everything being fucked.'

'Fuckin' oath! Let's go show them whose country this really is. I'm getting my flag.'

Jacko marches off with Jonno in tow, fired up as they charge out to their car and rip open the door. The sizzling of hot metal on their fingers fuels their rage. Red pulses under their skin and through the purple burns across their flesh. They snatch the flags out from under the car seats. A few empties clink as they fall off the flags and onto the torn car carpet.

The flag corners knot around their necks with ease. The red, white and blue, and the green and gold flap proudly out from their necks. Jonno and Jacko stand with fists on their hips once their costume is complete.

They march on, down to the beach where their fellow diggers await.

'My fellow Australians!' Jacko shouts from the top of the dune. A few heads twist around from under their shade next to where the cricket wickets fell and now rest. 'My fellow Australians. We are in grave danger!' More heads from their Australia Day party turn around and start sitting up. 'We face a very serious threat here today. There is a cult that threatens to harm us. It promotes only death and destruction and faggots. It almost overwhelmed us today but we have seen the light,' he slaps Jonno on the back. More of their entourage turn, a few begin to stand. A drunken fire kindles in some of them. Their purple, inked skin flushes with blood, ready to fight for their nation at the drop of a hat. 'These unStrayan traitors to our nation have invaded our lands. They steal our jobs. They spit on our traditions and pervert our very way of life. Those muzzos come here and try to make this land their new muzzo territory.'

'Yeah,' a couple of blokes grunt from the beach. They stumble as they step closer to Jacko and Jonno. More of their mates turn and stand to hear what Jacko has to say. Jacko's eyes twitch fanatically at the swelling pack of deadset fair dinkum ridgy-didge true blue dinky-di Aussies. 'Fuckin' muzzos!' a few of the pack add to the chorus.

'Those fuckers can't take our land from us. They don't

belong here. We do. This is our land!' Jacko yells over the gusts of wind. The bright red flush of his mounting rage looks like war paint. 'Let's show those fuckin' muzzos that this is good Australian land they've invaded. We'll make them too scared to bring their filthy ways here again. Who's with me?!'

'Fuck yeah!' the building crowd shouts.

'This is our land. We need to take it back! It's ours! Let's go get 'em. Aussie! Aussie! Aussie!'

'Oi! Oi! Oi!' the mob shouts back.

'Fuckin' oath let's get 'em,' Jonno shouts, his chest filling with pride.

Jonno and Jacko take the lead. They kick through the sand heading in the direction of the town square. A mob of thirty patriots follow their lead. Australian flags worn as capes flutter behind them, chasing them into their just cause.

CHRISTMAS IS COMING AROUND AGAIN. IT'S NEVER TOO EARLY TO PREPARE WITH OUR CHRISTMAS SPECIAL PACKAGES. COME IN STORE TO FIND HUGE DISCOUNTS ON ALL GIFTS AND CHRISTMAS SUPPLIES. YOU'LL FIND EVERYTHING YOU NEED AT GOOD PRICES TO KEEP YOUR FAMILY HAPPY AT CHRISTMAS. ASH-MART DEPARTMENT STORES. OPEN EVERY DAY EIGHT AM TO NINE PM.

Timmo

Timmo looks up from where he's bobbing in the shallows of the sea. His arse bounces roughly on the sand as each wave draws back out to sea. Tamie lies back next to him, her body moving serenely in time with the water. Behind them on a beach a crowd gathers in front of the toilet block. The people chant and punch their fists into the air.

Timmo looks amongst the crowd and spots Jonno and Jacko at the helm. They shout into the crowd, their faces wild for war. A glimmer of concern emerges in Timmo's eyes. Tamie glances up at Timmo, blissfully ignorant of the commotion beyond the lapping waves.

'What are you thinking about?' Tamie flirts.

Timmo nods towards the beach. Tamie pulls herself up, her bikini dragging across the wet sand. She jerks around and plants herself cross-legged facing the seething throng.

'I see Jacko and Jonno finally got their clothes back on,' Tamie laughs. 'I didn't realise fucking would be such a big high five moment for them.'

'I don't think it's funny,' Timmo stands up. Water drains noisily from his boardies. 'It looks like a lynch mob. All they're missing is pitchforks.'

'What? Why the hell would you say that?'

'Because they're cranked up. I've seen Jacko and Jonno get into all kinds of shit when they're like this. And now they've got a crowd cheering them on.'

Timmo kicks through the water—and the sand and the flies—as he makes his way up to the group. Movement ripples out from the crowd as it parts like a bogan red sea to allow their two leaders to head the march along the beach. Timmo sprints across the hard, wet sand. His chest heaves in his rush to get in front of the crowd, gritting his teeth through the pain of exertion. The sand flicks about wildly as he runs directly for his two friends.

'Jacko, Jonno, hold up,' he says out of breath. He holds his arms out to stop the leaders' march.

'What is it?' Jacko barks. 'We've got some illegals to bash.'

'Wait, what? Why?' Timmo puffs back.

'They're over here taking all our jobs. They're ruining our culture, they're ruining our country.'

'Yeah fuckin' muzzos!' the crowd shouts back.

'Come of it, man. You've never applied for a job in your life,' Timmo replies.

'Yeah, well why the fuck should I?!'

'Are you seriously going to do this? Do you really think this is a good idea?' Timmo asks, straightening up.

'Absolutely!' Jonno retorts, his eyes wide with mania. 'We need to protect what's ours. We created this country from nothing and we made this country awesome! We need to fight to keep it that way. Come on guys. Let's get 'em!'

'Wait, stop! That wasn't even a Muslim celebration we went past before,' Timmo pleads futilely. 'You're heading for an Aboriginal event!'

'Aussie! Aussie! Aussie!' the crowd chants. 'Oi! Oi! Oi!'

Jacko and Jonno are gone, the chanting of the crowd drowning out Timmo's cries as it flows forward like a river around a boulder. No one touches Timmo as they trek by.

'What's all that about?' Tamie asks once she catches up to Timmo.

'They're starting a riot. They're totally wasted, they have no idea what's going on, and they don't know who they're about to beat into.'

'Shit. What can we do?'

'We can't stop this from happening.' Timmo says. 'All we can do is call the police. I'm dead if they find out, but we can't do nothing. Come on, let's get to our phones and warn them a fight is about to break out.'

Grant

The black latex is slick with blood. A crushing blow to the ribs sends Grant's gimp sliding across the cement floor. Grant winces at his bleeding knuckles, then frowns at the spatter of blood on his favourite polo top. He strips off the shirt, his sweaty skin shining in the dull light of the garage. An erection strains uncomfortably against his shorts. The gimp's raging cock stands free of its prison, Grant had permitted its release in honour of the special occasion.

164

The gimp grimaces through the pain of ecstasy, crawling piteously up to its master to grasp onto one of his legs. Grant swings his leg back and boots it in the jaw. A soft orgasmic yelp escapes its mouth as a tooth skitters across the cement trailed by a tail of blood. Grant marches across the floor, fists at the ready. He grabs onto the gimp's throat and begins pounding his fist repeatedly into its face. Grant ignores the angry throb intensifying in his fingers, instead fixating on the gash in the gimp's lip that widens with each blow.

The gimp sighs, a strangely placid signal that it's reached its absolute climax. Grant holds back his fist, panting with exertion. He looks down at the pallid mess on the floor and releases his grip. He looks down into those grey, satisfied eyes.

'Perfect,' the gimp mouths through its bloody tongue. 'Thank you.' It nods toward the hammer in the corner of the room and smiles.

Grant's chest heaves with sorrow. *It's time*, he admits to himself. He trudges over to the hammer and brings it back to the twisted shape that waits on the floor. Swollen eyes tear with rapture.

'Goodbye, my best friend,' Grant says.

The hammer comes down hard on the gimp's skull, smashing through the bone in a hideous crack. Grant swings the hammer back, heedless of the blood and bone and chunks of gore. Without a second swing, his beloved pet falls limply to the ground, only twitches to attest its final moments.

Grant brings the hammer down again, and again, and again, driven by pain and rage and ecstasy. He keeps swinging and heaving as the rage fights for dominance of his psyche. After a final blow he looks down but can see nothing that he can recognise. A primal growl howls from his lungs and echoes in the bare room.

A click signals the release of the lock on the garage door.

'What was that?' Helen asks from the doorway.

Helen slips into the garage and locks the door behind her. She walks through the dim light tentatively, each step controlled, fastidiously avoiding the splatter. She spots the gimp's shattered remains sprawled across the cement.

'What the fuck do you call this mess?' Helen demands.

Grant turns to his wife. A fiery red flashes across his eyes.

'I told you to get rid of him, not crush him into pulp.'

'You're never satisfied are you?' Grant seethes.

'What?' Helen stands imperious.

Grant charges on his wife, the hammer clutched tightly in his hand. He knocks her to the ground with a savage blow across her jaw. She moans, but has lost the ability to form words.

'I could never please you,' Grant shouts over her mute pleas. 'I never wanted him gone, you made me do this. You bitch!'

Grant strikes down again with the hammer. Each blow

splintering a new bone, opening a new beautiful laceration. The final hammer strike penetrates the open wound of his wife's chest with a slop. Her corpse pulses a final time and stalls into a useless heap.

'Now you're as weak as you made me. I'm stronger now!' Grant growls. 'Stronger than you'll ever be again.'

LOOKING FOR THAT SOMETHING SPECIAL FOR THE ONE YOU LOVE? AT AUSTRALIAN JEWELLERS WE HAVE AN EXTENSIVE RANGE OF ONE-OF-A-KIND PIECES JUST RIGHT FOR THAT SPECIAL SOMEONE. SEND YOUR MESSAGE OF LOVE WITH ONE OF OUR UNIQUE AUSTRALIAN JEWELLERS WORKS OF ART. ASK OUR FRIENDLY STAFF ABOUT ALTERATIONS AND OUR EXCITING AUSTRALIAN JEWELLERS SUMMER RANGE. OPEN WEEKENDS AND PUBLIC HOLIDAYS.

Ronald

'Good evening, I'm Ronald Ray with your Today's Affairs news brief. Coming up at seven-thirty, Kylie Smith has an exclusive exposé that debunks the global warming myths flooding today's liberal media. Here's Kylie with more.'

'Thanks Ronald. Kylie Smith reporting. Traditional

jobs in energy production using natural resources are under threat from the long-term myth powered by green groups and the leftist lobbies. Coal, the source of our great country's prosperity, could soon be wiped out if we fail to act now.

'Today's Affairs has obtained an exclusive report from the Natural Energy Institute. The report proves that greens groups are directly responsible for the majority of global warming catastrophes in a conspiracy to demonise coal as a natural energy source.

'The report implicates several environmentalist organisations, including the movement of renewable energy companies onto the ASX and the green lobby's ability to prevent government spending on cleaner coal production as major factors in the cause of extreme natural disasters caused by climate change in Australia.

'Tonight Today's Affairs will air an exclusive interview with the managing director of the Natural Energy Institute, Toni Grabbit, who will expose more damage that greens groups continue to cause to the lives of the average Australian and their families. I'm Kylie Smith. Back to you, Ronald.'

'Can you believe it? Thank you Kylie. She will bring you more on that story tonight at seven-thirty. Also tonight, are kettles taking longer to boil? We'll ask the experts to lift the lid on this hot issue that would get any Australian steaming. I'm Ronald Ray. I look forward to seeing you tonight for Today's Affairs.'

Claire and David

David and Claire wrestle their bathers back into an acceptable position. Post sex-bliss flushes across their faces.

'Gosh we've drifted a bit,' Claire says looking back at the beach. The mass of umbrellas and portable marquees has receded to tiny dots far along the beach. 'We should swim back to shore. I reckon Tony would have another batch of margaritas ready by now.'

'Aww, come on, we don't have go back yet do we?' David replies. He slides a hand against the naked skin of her stomach. A shiver pulses cold across her body.

'What? Isn't twice enough for you for one day?' she asks while turning to paddle back in.

'Baby you know how I am. And besides, it's not like we have an opportunity like this very often.'

'I know, but I'm exhausted now. Maybe again later.'

David drops down into the water and starts stroking next to Claire. Their heads bob slowly up and down with the movement of the waves. A relaxed fatigue trembles through their muscles. A delayed spasm from the sex twitches out of David's leg. He smiles through the pleasure and keeps dragging himself through the water.

'Um, how are you going with swimming?' Claire asks.

'Pretty pooped actually,' David says.

'Me too,' an exhausted puff of air escapes Claire's mouth. 'And we don't seem to be getting any closer to shore.'

David quickly tries to gauge the distance to the shore. He senses a change in the water that forces the haze of pleasure to clear in his head. A shot of dread collides with his chest. They're not getting any closer. He starts dragging harder against the water. The cold weight of the depths sucks away his strength.

'We're in a rip,' he yelps. 'We have to get out of it.'

David splashes viciously at the water. Salt lashes his eyes. His arms flail in and out of the water in desperate search of forward movement.

'Oh shit!,' Claire wails. 'We can't panic. Let's just take a few deep breaths and we can get through this.'

Intermission: The haunting fable and its deceptive design to lure campers to safety

'I can't believe you spun those girls such a story about drop bears. It's such a stupid joke,' Anthony says.

'I know right. But did you see the looks on their faces,' Kevin laughs. 'I reckon they actually fell for it, too.'

Anthony glances around the camp site. Not much can be seen beyond the reach of the firelight. The breeze is cool against his skin. The scrubland campground was empty except for the two of them and the girls they had just terrorised. Anthony smiles. *So peaceful*, he thinks.

'Oh hi girls, everything okay?' Kevin asks. Anthony snaps back from his musing to see the two Swedish girls standing next to the fire and smiling. 'I thought we had scared you off.'

'But no of course,' Heidi says in a thick accent. 'We must go in tent to do girl things.'

Kevin throws an eager look at Anthony. Heidi moves closer to Kevin and sits down on the log next to him. Agnes

eases over to Anthony and sits close to him. The warmth
from her leg seeps across to his. Anthony smiles at her, looking deeply into her blue eyes.

'Good to see the drop bears didn't get you,' Kevin jokes.
The girls laugh. Anthony senses a nervous edge to their
tittering.

'Of course the—how you say—drop bears would not get
us,' Agnes says through her giggles.

Kevin yelps in agony. Anthony twists around. Heidi's
hand holds the handle of a knife plunged deep into Kevin's
abdomen.

'Kev!' Anthony yells. Bloody gurgles bubble out in
response. 'Crikey! What are you doing?!'

'We survive,' Agnes responds neutrally. 'Many thanks
for you to warn us kindly about the drop bears. Maybe we
cannot survive the attack of such vicious animals. But now
they will not be hungry. They will have you to eat and so we
will be safe.'

Agnes tugs a fishing knife from her belt and thrusts it
into Anthony's chest. Heidi starts to mutter instructions in
Swedish.

'Bugger me,' Anthony whispers.

PART V

Cassandra

'Good evening, I'm Cassandra Cummings with your 5CCB news update.

'Founders Bay residents are being instructed to initiate their wildfire survival plan as a sudden change in gusty winds is blowing an out of control fire directly toward the town. Emergency services say the sudden change has created a larger uncontrollable front and warn everyone not to drive into smoke even if you think you know the roads. If it's too late for you to leave police recommend you shelter yourself indoors or make your way to the school hall where an evacuation centre is being set up.

'In more local news, a race riot has taken over the town square in Founders Bay. Early reports say that members of a non-local white pride movement have attacked a local Indigenous event chanting anti-immigration epithets. Police are making their way to the scene.

'In other news, the local hospital is reporting a record number of people presenting with burns to their feet. A local hospital nurse told 5CCB the majority of people on the beach wear thongs or create their own temporary shade but some have spent prolonged periods standing barefoot on sand at temperatures up to forty-eight degrees Celsius, causing severe burns. Alcohol consumption is believed to also be a factor.

'Rolling blackouts have been reported in the Coonawarren district with many local businesses and homes affected. People are asked to check in on any elderly or vulnerable people who might be unable to escape the heat.

'In sport, the cricket will still go ahead on schedule despite forecasts showing the current heatwave extending for an extra few days. Cricket Australia assures 5CCB that extra water, shade and ice vests will be available for all players and spectators.

'To weather and it's not cooling down just yet with the temperature currently sitting on forty-two degrees. Hotter temperatures are expected for tomorrow.

'I'm Cassandra Cummings. Stay tuned to 5CCB for all breaking news on the wildfire emergency.'

Ronald

'Good evening. This is Ronald Ray for Today's Affairs. We interrupt Jamie and Marge's Cooking Juices to take you live to the scene of a race riot in the tourist town of Founders Bay. Local reporter Rachel Kind is on the scene. Rachel?'

'Watch it f****r. Thanks Ronald. This is Rachel Kind. I'm
here at Founders Bay where a peaceful Australia Day celebration has turned into a race riot. Sirens are ringing out behind
me. Smoke is rising all around the town square.

'The riot began when racial slurs were exchanged between
Muslim immigrants to the town and the local Indigenous
community. The verbal insults quickly escalated to violence
that has so far left five white Australians who were caught in
the crossfire dead from apparent knife wounds.

'Nowhere is safe in this town at the moment. This riot is
the most violent event this town has seen in its history. It is
unlikely that anyone will be safe from the impact of today's
ev—'

'Rachel? Rachel? Can you hear me? We appear to be
having some technical difficulty. We will have coverage back
up and running as soon as possible so that we can return
to the brave reporting of Rachel live at the coastal town of
Founders Bay. In the meantime we leave you to return to
Jamie and Marge's Cooking Juices. We'll be back breaking
the news for you. Until seven-thirty or when the real news
breaks, I'm Ronald Ray. Good evening.'

Timmo

Timmo mutters his frustration and drops his phone onto the
towel.

'How'd it go?' Tamie asks, dazed. She ogles the rising smoke that runs the length of the sky and out to sea. Her finger traces through the air chasing the beautiful filigree shapes in the clouds.

'Shit,' Timmo curses. 'Triple zero said that all personnel have been deployed to the fire already. If there isn't someone here in the next few minutes then there won't be for at least three hours.'

'Whoa, three hours,' Tamie echoes.

'You're still fuckin' high aren't you?' Timmo mutters. Tamie bursts into a fit of giggles. 'Goddamnit!'

'Right! Who called me?' A commanding voice asks from the top of the beach. Timmo jerks around to see a young police officer standing by himself. He scans the faces that turn with his voice with a look of dumb impatience creasing his face. Many onlookers quickly turn away. 'We're very busy. What the hell is that?' the officer barks sternly. He stares in the distance down the sand.

Timmo stands to get the officer's attention but the officer waves him off as he peers towards a commotion further down the beach. Timmo follows the officer's line of sight and spots a small group of naked men huddling together on the beach. The officer marches off determinedly.

'That's bloody great,' Timmo admits dejectedly. 'Just fantastic. Only one cop shows up to stop a riot and he's off to arrest some skinny dippers instead.'

Timmo plonks himself back down on the towel. The sun

dims, struggling to penetrate the thickening smoke, easing the strain on Timmo's reddened skin.

IN TONIGHT'S NEWS WE SPEAK TO FEDERAL SHADOW MINISTER FOR RECREATION, EDUCATION, CHILDHOOD MENTAL HEALTH, INDUSTRY, SCIENCE AND TECHNOLOGY DEVELOPMENT, THE MANAGER OF OPPOSITION BUSINESS, AND SPOKESPERSON FOR THE OPPOSITION LEADER WHILE HE'S ON HOLIDAYS THE HONOURABLE MEMBER CRYSTAL GREENWITH, WHO TODAY ANNOUNCED THE OPPOSITION'S POLICY ON ABORTION. GREENWITH DREW HUGE APPLAUSE WITH THE MAINLY FE-MALE CROWD WHEN SHE ANNOUNCED THAT THE OPPOSITION WILL HAVE NO PART IN TELLING WOMEN WHAT THEY MUST DO WITH THEIR BODIES. THE OPPOSITION, IF ELECTED, PLANS TO ROLL OUT A NATIONAL EDUCATION AND HEALTH PROGRAM DESIGNED TO EMPOWER WOMEN TO KNOW THEIR BODY, THEIR RIGHTS AND THE SERVICES THAT ARE AVAILABLE FOR THEM IN LINE WITH UNION POLICY. MORE TONIGHT AT SIX.

Grant's breaths heave deeply in his chest. A rising confidence broadens his shoulders. The hammer is poised tightly within his grip, the metallic head drips thick blood from the fleshy chunks caught in the claw. He stares down at the remnants of his wife. The white dress is splattered with hair and dark stains soaked with the last of her life.

Heated pride fuels a newly discovered power inside Grant. He feels the release of the shackles he had once begged for. The rush for domination pulsates red mist behind his eyes.

Grant steps toward the door with cold and calculated determination. The coolness of the door knob doesn't register in the palm of his hand. He unlocks the latch and pulls open the door. He steps out of the garage to a dark stillness in the house. The door stays open behind him, pulling some stale air back into the garage. He steps further out and notices the haze that hangs heavily over the house.

The power is out. None of the appliances drone with their usual buzzing. The lights remain dull. A darkness across the sky blocks the rays of the evening sun. The smoke floats ominously across the sky and out to sea. Silhouettes stalk the veranda, pointing at the sky and swaying side to side in a daze.

Grant recognises the shadows. Hatred for their presence

in his house sparks fury in his mind. The sight of Helen's family, reflections of who she was and her control over him, fill him with a fresh rage. He steps over to the sliding door and eases it open.

'I've never seen anything like it before,' Margaret gapes at the smoke. 'It's so thick.'

The hammer clangs heavily against the door frame. The group on the porch gaze around slowly, reluctant to turn away from the spectacle to divert their eyes towards Grant. They gasp. Margaret lets out a small shriek, hand covering her mouth like a typecast damsel. The sight of Grant in the doorway, splattered with blood, loathing in his eyes, drains the blood from their gaunt faces.

'Are you okay, Grant dear?' Aunt Liz asks, her shaking hand reaches out in a feeble attempt to help.

'Get off my property,' Grant seethes.

'What?' Zac stammers out.

'Get the FUCK off my property!'

They all step back in fright. Grant's armed hand rises ready to strike.

'Whe—where's Helen?' Margaret cries.

Grant stares her down. He catches Margaret's eyes. Beneath the glistening fear swelling in her eyes Grant spots the same shade of control Helen had. The disgust of being under someone's control again pumps through him. He steps aggressively toward Margaret. She squeals and runs out onto the path outside of the house. Her family dashes after her. The dark shade across Grant's face confirms for them the worst fate for Helen.

Zac pulls out his Samsung Galaxy and starts dialling triple zero. Grant howls and charges forward. The family cries out and runs further down the beach, towards the car park. Grant steps up to the edge of the patio and balances firmly on the end paver. He watches Zac fumble and pull the phone up to his ear. Around them the grey smoke thickens with wheezing gasps of ash and eucalyptus. *Nothing can touch me now*, Grant thinks to himself, chest puffing. *I am free and alone.*

'I CONTROL MY OWN PETS NOW!' he bellows over the wind.

Keith

Keith stands uselessly on the back of the fire truck watching the destruction sprawl before him. The truck rests on a lean. A hose gargles through the humming of the pump as it sucks muddy water from the dam. Gusts of wind burn the back of his neck above his high collar. Plumes of smoke gush angrily out of the sizzling scrub. A premature darkness creeps over the town as the fire bears down on it.

Keith shakes his head. Feebleness numbs his body. The flames teeter at the edge of the town. Keith sighs in defeat. *All the elections, all the volunteer work and all the time spent*

*working the fields to provide for this town are being laid
to waste,* he thinks. *We have only one truck. The roads are
blocked. The fire has changed direction. We're alone with pole
spectator's position.*

Keith

What is it all for? Keith thinks to himself. He holds onto the
metal edging of the truck. The buzzing of the pump continues in the back of his mind. *Everything I have. Everything
I've ever had is about to be burned away. My homestead might
be safe. But what of Dot? What of Ralph? I can't help them
now. I can barely get us out of this paddock without driving
through the flames. At least the wind change protected us out
here. Small consolations.*

*Has anyone called for help in the town? Can anyone
actually get in to help them? Sarge would have been flat out
working the roads and keeping people away from the smoke.
Maybe the holiday transfers will keep everyone safe.*

Dot. My Dot. I hope you are safe. I pray that you're back

home already whipping up another delicious pie or roast for our traditional Australia Day dinner. I know our house is safe for now. God I hope you're there.

Keith's face drops. The skin around his eyes droops into an unnaturally old swing. The red rings flush with tears. His confident demeanour evaporates.

Why do we even bother? his thoughts overflow with doubt and resigned anger. *We are nothing but small men. The big men in Canberra don't care about us as long as we're busy doing our own thing. The country turns against us and its godforsaken climate is a mongrel and they gut our budgets because they think we're doing too well. We were safe. Now we have no resources and the town is burning. The money might as well burn with the town. We need trucks and people but by the time they accept that fact it's too late. Don't fix what's not broken I guess.*

Anger pumps into his heart. The useless rage stands with greater stature in him. He grips tighter onto the edge of the truck ready for the vehicle to move again.

Nicholas

Nicholas sits in the shallows of the surf watching the flashes of orange behind the houses. Dark grey clouds billow out from the flickering flames. The fire seems so close from his spot on the beach. *I hope everyone is alright*, he thinks.

Nicholas looks across the beach. In front of him a cluster of people lie passed out on their towels. Their marquees that flap against the increasing breeze can barely maintain their weak grip onto the sand. Purple-red skin marks their drunken slump on the white sand. Those bogans still awake stare weakly at the flames glowing behind the buildings. Their heads sit slumped against a towel and slowly lift as their interest peaks and wanes through their slumber.

Further down the beach Nicholas sights a group of naked men. From the distance not much is clear beyond the fact that they don't have any clothes on. They gather around something on the ground. Nicholas squints for focus. A body lies flat on the sand, the men stand around looking panicked and dazed.

A muffled cry screams over the wind from behind Nicholas. He twists around and rebalances against the waves. The gentle lapping of the warm seawater drags like a massage over his ankles. He hears the muffled shout again. Scanning the horizon he sees an arm wave in the distance. He pushes into the sand and pulls himself up higher. The sand sinks under the extra pressure of his weight. The pooled water in his boardies pulls downwards on the velcro. He sees the hand again waving helplessly from the water, and catches sight of two dots as they bob up and down in the distance. An occasional splash sprays up next to their heads as they shrink into the expanse around them.

The cold realisation trembles through Nicholas. *They're*

in a rip, Nicholas's mind darts through the options. *They need help*, he thinks. He turns quickly in the water. No options lay amongst the drunken corpses on the beach. *They might have a phone*, Nicholas thinks, kicking the water aside so he can get to the beach.

'I CONTROL MY OWN PETS NOW!' growls across the wind.

The powerful war cry howls down across the sand. Nicholas's head snaps up toward the culprit. Futility smothers him. His dad stands on the porch, a hammer hanging from his hand, his mouth wide open with each roar of defiance. Dark red spatters coat his dad's skin. Nicholas collapses down onto the sand. Any energy left in his body seeps out of him making way for fear and despair. A sunburnt guy leans up from the towel next to a giggling girl to stare at Nicholas's screaming father.

Claire

'I think he saw us,' Claire gasps above the deepening waves. 'David? David?'

Claire strains her neck around in the water. Nothing but the hills and valleys of the waves are within her sight.

'David!' she splutters to no one.

Claire drags her body around in the water. Her arms ache with each stroke. The beach is distant now. She can no longer see the figure on the beach that she thought might have seen them. In a desperate reach she grips her hand randomly in the water. Bubbles squirt out of her fist as she grasps at empty water. Nothing firm catches in her hand.

Claire's muscles weaken beyond the point of helping someone else. Her stomach aches from the tension of keeping her chin out of the water. The water continues to drift her further out into the deep.

'David,' she whimpers.

IN THIS WEEK'S INDEPENDENT WEEKLY, BILLIONAIRE PLAYBOY DICK ROGERS HAS APPEARED IN COURT FOR THE EIGHTH TIME UNDER CORRUPTION CHARGES. HE SPOKE TO CAMERAS SUPPORTED BY HIS SIXTH WIFE NADIA TASSEL BEFORE ENTERING THE COURT ROOM. HE TOLD REPORTERS HE HAS DONE NOTHING WRONG AND LOOKS FORWARD TO THE END OF THE WITCH HUNT WHEN HIS INNOCENCE WILL BE PROVEN BEFORE THE FEDERAL COURT. INDEPENDENT WEEKLY. OUT NOW.

Jane and Danielle

Danielle groans herself awake. A boozy cloud sits as a rising fog on her mind.

'Eeeerrr,' she complains. 'Why does my arsehole hurt so much? Did I shit myself?'

Jezza and Derek high-five each other by the window. Danielle lifts her head and spots Jane on the floor, fully dressed and rolling around with her hands around her stomach. The blokes stand looking at something in the palm of their hand. At regular intervals they slap each other on the back. Danielle moans and rolls herself onto her back. A fresh breeze soothes around her bare skin like water to a burn.

'Oh my god, I can't believe you did that. That's awesome,' Jezza holds up another hand for Derek to high-five.

Danielle squints her eyes at the small device in Jeremy's hand. She recognises it as an iPhone as the fog lifts more from her sight. The sound in the room ricochets between the cheers from Jezza and Derek and distorted grunts from the iPhone speakers. Danielle pushes herself up onto her elbows. The breeze on her vagina and arse becomes more prevalent. The coolness of the exposure draws her back into the reality of the room. She looks down upon herself and cringes. Nothing is covering her.

The haze drops completely from her view. The hunt for clothing aggressively powers her. Her bikini bottom lies next to her on the bed. She snatches at it and shoves her legs through the strings.

'What are you guys watching,' Danielle slurs as she forces herself off the bed, bikini top in hand and stumbles over to

Jezza and Derek.

The blokes smile with pride down at the screen in Jeremy's hand. They don't even flinch as Danielle sways up next to them. She glances down at the screen to the video streaming.

'What, porn?' Danielle laughs to herself.

Danielle looks down at the film of a bright, white arse from the hips down thrusting into a woman who barely moves on the bed.

'I've seen covers like that before,' Danielle's mouth drops.

She looks closer at the screen. Buried in the comfort of the pillow she sees the side of a face she spends a lot of time caring for. Her unconscious face rests against the pillows in the video. The film bounces around more than the thrusting into her. She focuses her eyes on the show before them. Her hips are perched up and bare against the crotch of the guy pushing deeper into her. A draft of prickles rise up around her rear.

Danielle smacks the phone out of Jezza's hand and slaps him over the back of the head with her open palm.

'What the fuck?' Derek complains. 'I can't replace the screen again without voiding the warranty.'

'Did you fuck me up the arse?' Danielle shouts through her newfound clarity. She punches Derek in the shoulder. 'That's not on. That's an exit, not an entrance. I was happy to do whatever for the drinks but I'm a woman, nothing goes in my arse.'

Danielle unleashes a sudden burst of strength. Her nails sink into the side of Jezza's face and drags through the weathered skin. Jezza yelps as the flesh is torn from his cheek. Blood drips instantly from the scratch marks on his face.

'What the fuck was that for?' Jezza hisses.

'You fucking raped me up the fucking arse!' Danielle shouts back.

'Bitch you wanted it. You didn't object,' Derek jumps to his mate's defence.

'It's hard to object when you're fucking unconscious,' Danielle turns on Derek. She curls her fist and swipes it clean against the side of his head. Her knuckles throb as blood rushes to the bruised fingers. She shakes the pain out of her hand.

'What the fuck is wrong with you?' Jezza says, his hand covering half his face. 'If you didn't want it then why did you take our drinks?'

'I was up for a whole heap of fun with you guys, but I have to be in on the game too. I could've given you a gobby if you wanted. Even rim you if that's what you're into. But I'm not being fucked up the arse!' Danielle declares.

Danielle steadies her footing on the carpet with a smoothness of motion that comes naturally to her. She poises herself on one leg and swings forward with the other. The top of her foot crunches into the squishy spot between Jezza's legs. The instant pain knocks him to the ground as a wave of nausea swims up into his stomach with a throbbing he can't control.

'What the fuck man!?' Derek shouts.

Derek reaches down and grabs Jezza under his arm and struggles to drag him to the door.

'Fuckin' crazy bitch. Get your head right,' Derek grumbles as he lifts Jezza and their Esky out the door. Jezza gasps and gags on the rising vomit. The sound of his retching disappears down the stairs.

'What was that about?' Jane moans while lifting herself up onto the bed.

'They fucked me up the arse,' Danielle shakes her hand at the door behind them.

'Serves them right,' Jane groans. 'They should know a woman deserves better. Just because they gave us drinks doesn't mean they can fuck us up the arse.' Jane squints at Danielle. 'Gosh, you look like your mum right now. Creepy.'

On this #AustraliaDay let's not forget the true history of this country. It's 1000s of yrs old. Not a few hundred.

Tracey Goldwin, Drew Kelly and 42 others like this

Simon, Tony and their guests cluster close to each other. Water still beads on their naked bodies. Sam lies still on the beach, gritty with sand. Michael squats down again and presses his finger against Sam's throat one more time. Nothing under the surface moves. The expression of wit and charm in Sam's features fades as his jaw slackens. A dimly peaceful look of sleep creeps over his façade.

'What do we do now?' Tony croaks out.

'There's nothing we can do,' Simon answers quietly, his head shaking. 'We've called the ambulance, but the roads are closed due to the fire. All we can do now is wait here with him until someone comes.'

'Should we cover him up?' Michael suggests. 'Just for basic decency.'

'NOBODY MOVE!' a bellowing voice behind them commands. 'I HAVE DRAWN MY WEAPON. EVERYONE PLACE THEIR HANDS ON THEIR HEADS AND TURN AROUND SLOWLY.'

The group of nude men shiver from cold fright. Simon raises his hands as smoothly as his shuddering allows and turns around to expose himself to the controlling voice behind them. He spots a young police officer standing ten feet away with his pistol drawn. The rest of the group turn just as carefully, leaving Sam's body ignored on the beach. The officer visibly cringes at the sight before him.

'I knew I'd have my work cut out for me when I was called to a riot but I didn't suspect this,' the officer mutters. 'What's wrong with him on the ground?' he shouts. No one offers to respond instantly. 'Why isn't he moving? Too pissed?'

Matt eases himself to the front of group. The loose flabs of his skin tense in his stomach. The wet greying hair on his chest stretch as the muscles clench.

'I'm a lawyer,' Matt calmly states.

'I don't give a fuck who you are,' the officer points his gun directly at Matt's chest. 'I just want to know what's wrong with the guy on the ground.'

'He's dead,' Matt's eyes drop as he says those words out loud. The officer's face tenses further, anger creases into his eyelids.

'What did you fuckers do to him? What's happening here? What did you do?'

'Just calm down,' Matt says. He holds his palms out for the officer to see. 'We were swimming. He was stung by a jellyfish. We tried to help him, but I guess he went into cardiac arrest. We're the ones who called for help.'

'Why would you call in help for your own queer riot fuckin' mardi gras shit?' the officer's eyes dart around as if surrounded by predators. 'That's it. Everyone lie on the sand. Hands behind your backs. NOW!'

'Okay,' Matt says. 'We'll do what you ask. Come on guys. Everything is going to be okay. Everyone just do what the officer says. He looks new and a little on edge.'

'On edge? What does he think we are at the moment?' Tony hisses.

'SHUT UP! And lie down,' the officer demands.

'Just do it,' Matt instructs while lying himself face first in the sand and placing his hands behind his back. He cringes as the heat still in the sand presses on his scrotum.

The rest of the group follow his example. Michael glances steadily from the officer, to the ground and back to the officer. The gun shakes alarmingly in their direction. The officer steps awkwardly side to side on the sand, waiting for the men to be vulnerable on the ground.

The officer flashes a look over to the body on the sand. The pallid complexion and lifeless posture seem to pose no threat in the officer's mind. He turns his attention to the line-up of men pressing their chins into the sand.

'Right. Nobody move. I'm going to tie all of your hands up and then I'll proceed to interrogate you,' the officer says hesitantly. 'If anyone resists I'll be forced to use pepper spray or my Taser. This is your only warning.'

The officer reaches into his vest with trembling hands and retrieves a bundle of plastic ties. One by one the men groan as their hands are tightened together with zip ties.

'You can't do this,' Simon protests.

'What was that?' The officer pulls out his Taser.

Simon sinks further into the sand. The threat of the Taser shatters any confidence he had remaining.

A hiss breaks out in the scrub at the head of the dunes. The officer jumps back, firing the Taser in the direction of the noise. The prongs crackle into the sand. Electricity ticks as the Taser fires uselessly into the grains of sand on the beach. The officer drops his Taser with a light thud.

'Oh shit,' the officer gasps. 'We have to get out of here.'

Matt turns his head to look up at the officer. Orange sparkles in his eyes as he stares in fright at a growling beast in the nature strip at the top of the beach.

CHRISTMAS IS COMING AROUND AGAIN. IT'S NEVER TOO EARLY TO PREPARE WITH OUR CHRISTMAS SPECIAL PACKAGES. COME IN STORE TO FIND HUGE DISCOUNTS ON ALL GIFTS AND CHRISTMAS SUPPLIES. YOU'LL FIND EVERYTHING YOU NEED AT GOOD PRICES TO KEEP YOUR FAMILY HAPPY AT CHRISTMAS. ASH-MART DEPARTMENT STORES. OPEN EVERY DAY EIGHT AM TO NINE PM.

Simon

The officer makes a run for it. His boots pound heavily over the sand as he sprints away from the encroaching flames.

'What the hell was that? Is he just going to leave us here?' Michael says.

'Fucking newbies,' Matt curses. 'He's probably been moved between stations ten times. They're the reason obvious criminals get off. Bloody negligence.'

'Holy shit,' Tony whispers.

Tony's eyes rise up from the sand to the snarling wall of flame bearing down on the beach. The others wriggle across the sand at the sight of the wildfire edging on the sand. Tony lifts his head. A sudden radiant heat slaps him across the face.

'Argh,' he groans. 'It's fuckin burning us already. We have to get out of here.'

'How? We're tied up,' Tony cries.

'Worm it on your guts,' Michael suggests. 'If you can get your hands under your feet to get your arms back we should be able to get out of here quickly.'

'Can't. The tag is too tight,' Simon groans. A red ring of blood cuts in his skin under the tag. He yelps through the agony and pushes his body through the sand with his legs. He digs his knees into the sand in an attempt to stand up. The sand's grip gives way under his weight, flopping him back onto his belly.

The group of men struggle against the sand and heat searing across their backs. Their flesh grates against the increasingly coarse sensation of the beach.

'What about the water?' Michael shouts, his eyes

drooping ready to faint in the heat.

'We can't swim like this and the jellies could be there still,' Matt yells back.

'I'll take a sting over roasting alive any day of the week,' Simon yells. 'We've got to try something.'

The wildfire pops and sizzles as trunks burst and sap explodes. The flames bite at the edge of the sand. The wind screams overhead bearing the intense heat down on top of them, and along with it burning chunks of debris that land amongst the desperate men. Tony searches around wildly as he seeks escape from the burning coals near him as the beach becomes a minefield. Michael rolls away from the glowing embers as the heat burns his skin.

'It's the wind,' Michael screams. 'It's carrying the burning scrub onto us. It's so hot. I can feel my skin blistering.'

The howling wind continues its rain of fire. Glowing embers fizz and crackle as they pound down on the beach around the men.

'We have to go faster,' Matt directs.

The group twist and flap themselves along the beach as fast as their muscles can convulse. The wind picks up, blasting heat directly down onto the sand. The men cry under its intensity. An unnatural screech escapes Matt's lungs as a burning branch lands on his back. The flesh bubbles into dark blisters. He rolls on the sand to remove the coals from his spine. The tumbling on the sand is futile as each roll presses the embers deeper into his skin.

'Matt!' Other Sam shouts.

Matt's flailing slows. His eyes no longer struggle through the pain. The intense shock of the burn tumbles his body into a pleasant numbness. Simon starts a commando charge to help Matt. His assistance is cut short as a lump sears down into the side of his leg. His scream is drowned out as a clump of ash and burning wood tumbles into the side of his face. Tony stretches his face out of the way as far as he can but his path across the beach is blocked.

The echoes of screams erupt from the naked men as the debris rains down fiercely. The asteroid crackle of embers hails down to a chorus of yelps and pleas. Flesh barbecues and pops from the searing heat. Clumps of superheated sand are caught on the wind and scatter over the naked bodies, covering the men with burning granules from head to foot. Even as the agonised screams start to fade, the firestorm gets heavier and pelts them with more missiles. Their naked bodies drop limp and idle on the sand. Blisters on their skin burst with the sudden rush of heat as they are covered deeper in an onslaught of falling cinders from the bushfire.

Underneath the cloying stink of ash and perfumed incense of eucalyptus rises the sickly-sweet aroma of roasting meat.

'What the fuck's happening out there?' Jane moans from the windowsill. 'Everyone is shitting themselves as if Godzilla is coming.'

'Wait, isn't that my dad?' Danielle points down as she reaches the window.

A bloodied man patrols back and forth on the edge of the property next door. Footmarks scrape across the boundary as Grant relentlessly marches. Every few steps he shouts down at the people on the beach.

'Yeah looks like it. What's he doing with a hammer?' Jane asks.

Jane fiddles at the window and yanks on the metal frame.

'Goddamnit, it's locked. He won't be able to hear me from here,' Jane says.

'But what about them?' Danielle says pointing at the people rushing about on the beach. Several sink themselves backwards into the surf. They drop down to their necks in the water and hold wet towels up over their heads. 'Something big is going down and we need to find out what it is.'

'Who cares,' Jane drops the curtain and flops herself onto the bed. 'My head is throbbing and I can barely stand up. You sure taught me a thing or two. I think I'm still getting drunk as we speak. How much did we down?'

'Dunno,' Danielle replies, carefully placing herself on the

bed next to Jane.

'OMG LOL,' Jane convulses with laughter at the sight of Danielle grimacing when her arse touches the bed covers. 'You've never gone there before?'

'Never!' Danielle snaps back. 'The least he could've done was use more lube,' she groans.

'So, what was it like?' Jane asks. 'Were they big?'

'I don't know. I was out of it. That beer made my day, though. I don't think I could have lasted the day with our family.'

'I don't think your dad could either. What's with that?'

'Who knows?' Danielle sighs and lowers herself onto her back. 'He probably grew a pair and told your family to get fucked. They always drive him mad but he never speaks up. Mum owns him.'

Jane sniffs vaguely at the air.

'What's that smell?' she asks.

'You mean other than sex and piss?' Danielle mutters back.

'No. Yes. I smell smoke.'

'Probably weed then. Who knows what these bogans do?'

Jane slides off the edge of the bed. She straightens the straps on her bikini as she rises onto the carpet. The acrid smell of smoke fills her nose as she reaches standing height.

'No I can seriously smell smoke, like house fire smoke,' Jane says.

'Then go check it out,' Danielle replies. She shuts her
eyes as another drunken wave washes over her mind.

Jane steps carefully across the carpet to the door. The
reek of smoke intensifies as she reaches the door. She stares
down at the gold handle on the door as a wisp of smoke
slithers out of the lock. Jane shakes her head in disbelief.
Her hand latches onto the handle and yanks the door open.
A blast of heat bursts through the door.

'What the?' Danielle gasps.

Black clouds and radiant heat singe the room with glee.
The girls' cry for help chokes in their lungs. The dust and
smoke smothers their faces in a burning embrace. They flop
to the ground, defeated. Danielle squeezes out a prayer
to pass out quickly. The flood of billowing black smoke
through the room answers her prayers. They cough their last
breath as the house burns around them.

Timmo

'Get up Tamie, get up now,' Timmo shakes Tamie out of her
tired giggles.

She stirs from the towel and crinkles her nose at the
burning air.

'What the hell is that smell? Did you fart?' she asks.

Timmo grabs onto her shoulder and roughly twists her
around to face the beachfront houses as they burst into

flames. The tumbledown shack on the end blazes completely alight. Tamie gulps down a fragile panic rising from her chest. She clamps down onto her chest and huddles over away from the blasting heat.

'What do we do?' Tamie cries.

Timmo scans the beach. The flames run the length of the town. They can't stand without the heat disorienting them. The smoke smothers the view around the town.

'Into the water,' he directs spotting the only clear path out of there. 'Grab your towel. Quick!'

As Tamie and Timmo crawl across the clumps of sand they're chased by the crackling cacophony of the fire behind them. The water laps out to greet Tamie and Timmo as they retreat into its shallows, submerging themselves up to their necks.

'Soak your towel and throw it over your head,' Timmo says.

They push their towels completely under the water until the weight drags the fabric down. Timmo whips his out and swings it over his head. The towel smacks heavily on his head before the edges settle in the water. The cave around his head blocks his view but holds back the heat from the fire. Around them he sees others crawl into the water for protection. The second house sizzles alight. Timmo's head drops knowing his father's house will soon be in flames too.

Grant

Grant pauses in his patrol along the front of his yard. The crowd is gone. His manly shadow has cast fear into their hearts. He grins knowing he successfully defended his land. His fearlessness grows with a rising sense of invincibility.

The hammer hangs loosely in his hand as he turns and stomps back up into the house. A black haze floats around him as he walks forth, determination bestowing him with a tunnel vision that leads him directly where he needs to go. The stifling heat around him is disguised under the blanket of superiority settling over his thoughts.

The door to the garage creaks open, greeting Grant with a dank stench. Grant flicks at the light switch uselessly out of habit. Two unrecognisable shadows sprawl across the floor in front of him, their juices intermingling in the middle of the room.

Grant stares down at both piles of tangled limbs. The dirty white fabric of the lump near the door stirs a fresh hatred inside him, and his grip tightens on the hammer as he prepares to act out his rage. But in the gloom he catches a flash of shiny black latex from the far corner of the room. The silhouette of his beloved pet lying mangled and peaceful calms Grant, soothes his contempt for the beast lying next to him on the floor. Grant drops his hammer, all malice forgotten, the metal squashes the remains of Helen's nose.

Grant's hand slides gently under the limp body of his pet. The latex grips against his fingers as he reaches under the pet's thin bones. He pulls the slight weight into himself, and weeps. The pain is uncontrollable. Grant's body rocks as waves of anguish escape into the stale air. Still lost in his grief and tenderness, Grant fails to register the thickening smoke chasing him into the garage. He sobs, actively ignorant of the world around him. Grant chokes through tears, and then through smoke, determined to remain in the peaceful companionship his pet had offered him over the years.

'Go back to where you came from!' Jacko chants into the incited mob.

Jeers shout back at Jacko over the scuffles in the town square. Jonno bounces nearby, each drop-kick he unleashes smashes into the brown bastard that lies unmoving on the ground.

Jacko shivers with the tight little thrill of destruction. The urge to hurt them more dances in the forefront of his mind. His eyes dart around in search of a target. He spots groups of patriots punching into a muzzo they've singled out. But that's no good to him, that situation is already sorted and there's nothing more for him to contribute. His mind races with the possibilities of how he can further their cause.

Then before him he sees three flagpoles rise like monumental pillars against the dark sky. In the centre stands a symbol he recognises. The Australian flag flickers like a beacon, but is under siege by two other flags, a green and blue eyesore grasps at the edge of the Southern Cross while some red, black and yellow abomination obscures the Union Jack.

Jacko marches towards the flag poles with an insatiable feeling of strength. A flying brick that slams into the side of his leg doesn't penetrate the patriotic determination controlling his thoughts. He lines up the nearest pole, grabs onto the rope and untangles the knot that fastens the flag in place. The flag steadily descends as Jacko tugs the rope, and as soon as the blue and green flag hits the ground Jacko unclips it. Jacko repeats this feat on the opposite side and pulls the flag to the ground with little difficulty.

With two flags clumped under his arm Jacko strides out into an open patch within the town square, empty except for a limp bouncy castle and a pine tree. He dumps the fabric onto the ground in an awkward clash of colours and spits on them in contempt. He rips on the velcro in his pants and pulls out his cock to complete the insult to these migrant invaders. He pisses on the flags, the colours darkening with the yellow stream of liquid.

'What the hell are you doing man?' Jezza asks from behind Jacko. Jacko snaps his head around. Derek stands next to him rubbing a fresh bruise on his face. Jonno spots the fresh cuts on Jezza's face too and bounds over to inspect the war wounds.

'I'm fighting against the migrants' fuckin' attempt to invade our country with their halal and bullshit religions. Women should wear as little as they want!' Jacko says.

'And how is pissing on the Aboriginal flag helping you to do that?' Jezza wonders aloud.

'Nah mate,' Jacko insists. 'They're muzzo flags.'

'Nope. You fucking idiot.'

'Yeah, well they're still not Australian flags, are they?' Derek points out. 'Let's burn the bastards anyway.'

Jacko's eyes light up with an intense joy.

'You got a fuckin' lighter?' he asks. His eyes bulge with mania.

'Nope,' Derek answers. 'Hold on.' Derek turns to the pursuing mob of proud Australians. 'Oi! We need a lighter!' he shouts.

Three small coloured tubes are hurled at them on command. Derek picks one up and sparks a flame.

'I have one now. You got any petrol?'

'Shit,' Jacko says. 'Who the freakin' hell has petrol round here.'

The wind howls over their yells. The smoke embellishes the sky with another smother of grey soot. Gusts drive through the town square in a fury of heat and despair. A hollow crack startles the trio.

'What the fuck was that?' Jacko asks.

The aged pine tree fails under the constant beating of the hot wind. The branches cast a dull shadow across the square on its descent toward the sea. Jezza looks up and points uselessly at the tree. The weight of the trunk crashes down on the group holding the piss-stained flags. The smaller branches snap under the force of the fall, the thicker branches hold their own, skewering their soft flesh in multiple places.

Jonno looks up at the pandemonium of the fallen tree. Somewhere in all of that he thought he heard his name. He picks his way through the smoke across the town square. He can't make out much among the tangle, until some movement catches his eye. Among the branches, suspended like bloody puppets, hang Jacko, Jezza and Derek.

'Holy fuck.'

Mark

Mark presses the cold steak against his eye, feeling lucky there was even one left after all the sales and giveaways. In the shadows he sees his manager nursing a bruised leg and elbow. At the far end the rival manager presses a bag of frozen peas to his jaw. An eerie calm fills the shopping centre. The few customers caught inside sit uncomfortably at their café tables, sipping on thickshakes. An occasional awkward drag scratches out from under their metallic chairs.

'Now what?' Mark asks.

'We wait until the power comes on and then cut all our prices down to one dollar,' his manager responds. The pain throbs in his knee as he talks.

'Seriously, we're trapped in here and you're worried about discounted prices?' Mark complains.

'Yeah, of course. It's my job. I do what Head Office tells me to do. That's how things work at Ash's if you want to get anywhere.'

'How about getting out the front doors?' Mark shouts.

'Head Office forced centre management to install those

doors, huh? Did they say that when everything goes to shit it should just lock everyone in?'

'Calm down,' his manager waves his hand at Mark. 'Of course it was Head Office who organised all of this. They wanted to make sure that if someone cut the power to pull off a heist the doors would seal and keep them locked in.'

'Heist of groceries! What the hell man!?' Mark shouts. 'If they steal anything let them have it. If they run off with a box of condoms there's no need to shut down the whole building. Just claim it on insurance.'

'Head Office likes to send a message,' his manager says calmly.

'Wait. Whose Head Office?' Mark asks.

'Both of our Head Offices,' the rival groans across the plaza. 'They're one and the same.'

'What?' Mark turns on his manager. 'Is that true?'

'I suppose,' his manager shrugs. 'Depends on how you look at it. Both individual companies are owned by the same conglomerate. But they promote competition to build better business performance.'

'You're kidding me? We've been falling for that crap for years?'

'Well, I suppose,' the manager concedes. 'That information is on a need to know basis. We only found out by chance because of the building issues with this shopping centre. The executive managers had to step in and tell the builders what to do when they were setting everything up.'

Mark leans back onto the glass of the main entrance into Ash's. The doors don't budge, awaiting the override of the emergency shutdown.

'So, because one company had issues here every single door is locked so that no one can escape with any tiny piece of shit from the supermarket, which we were pretty much giving away anyway?'

'Not exactly, not every door,' the manager answers through a cringe. He moves to settle himself against a support rail near the Ash's entrance.

'What is that supposed to mean?' Mark glares at his manager.

'Isn't it obvious? Not every door shuts.'

'Fuck you,' Mark sighs. 'Which ones?'

'The tradesmen's roof access doors don't lock, the ones the tradies use to access the signs, to replace the lights and stuff.'

Mark stretches himself up off the pavers. He dusts the dirt and cigarette ash off his pants and heads toward the utility stairs hidden next to the delivery entrance of Ash's.

'Where are you going?' the manager asks from the floor.

'I'm getting out of here to see what the hell is going on. I reckon the whole town is in a blackout. The power's probably all sucked up by the air conditioners in this shit heap.'

Mark's scuffed black shoes clank on the metal steps as he works his way up the stairs. The thin steps remind him of a ladder more than a set of stairs. *Bloody Head Office*, he thinks. *Probably didn't want this classified as a dangerous ladder requiring training before using it. Bloody Head Office. If I wasn't so desperate to make rent and buy food, I'd tell them to fuck off. What sort of idiots would want to waste so much energy keeping in petty thieves? The worst thing people steal from a supermarket is a carton of Gillette razors. And it's not even always the good ones. What the hell is that smell? Is it getting hotter? These stairs must be more of a workout than I expected.*

Mark reaches the final rung on the stairs. He grabs roughly onto the handle and shoves open the lump of wood that is the door. The smell of smoke flushes across his face. His nose cringes at the reek of ash. He steps out onto the roof. A clear path of flat Colorbond is all that stands between him and freedom. Mark steps firmly out onto it.

SALE! SALE! SALE! THE OWNERS OF CARS AND CARS HAVE GONE MAD AND PUT EVERY VEHICLE ON SALE! GET TO A DEALERSHIP QUICKLY BEFORE THEY COME TO THEIR SENSES. HATCHBACKS! SEDANS! LIMOUSINES! EVERY CAR HAS GOT TO GO! SALE! CARS! MADNESS!
FOR A LIMITED TIME ONLY. CASH PURCHASES ONLY. PRICES SUBJECT TO CHANGE. AVAILABILITY VARIES BETWEEN LOCATIONS.

More gusts threaten to unbalance Mark as he navigates the thin strip of metal. The heat penetrates straight through his shirt and onto his skin. He ignores the instant sweat seeping out of his armpits and stands up straight and surveys the town around him.

Darkness covers the entire township, more than any blackout could explain. A billowing smoke cloud bellows out of a blaze stretching the length of the town. An orange snarl bares its teeth in a hideous grin around the edge of the town. Mark's heart sinks into his stomach. The rushing butterflies he had climbing to the roof died on the moment his eyes caught onto the sight around him.

Mark glances down to the town square near the shoreline. The ugly pine tree lies flat on the ground. Groups of people swing their fists and feet into each other, some of the redder battlers wearing the Australian flag like a cape. The wildfire has burned through the scrub all the way to the beach and engulfed the small strip of beachfront houses. People everywhere are panicking, except the countless bodies that lie still, unmoving.

The vision sickens Mark. He spins around to see the slim clear patch of the town. Dots of people rush about their backyards hosing down their roofs and gardens.

Mark slams his eyes shut and turns back to the centre of the town. Tears seep out the corners of his eyes. Resigned, he lowers his head to look away from the town.

Mark steps back into the shopping complex and eases the door shut behind him. The steps down to the plaza drag on as his shoes clink onto the thin metal. The solid bricks arrive too soon under the pressure of his foot. The bland shadow of the shopping complex surrounds him.

'How is it out there Mark?' his manager asks.

Mark drags himself back over to the entrance of the supermarket. He drops his face into his knees and wraps his head inside of his hands.

'Mark. What's happening outside? Is there a blackout for everyone else?' the manager insists.

'Happy Australia Day,' Mark whimpers.

Cannibalised Australia

Welcome to Australia Day, one of many national days dedicated to celebrating and commemorating our achievements. However, underneath the revelry the day is rife with political tension and white pride lurking to bark down anyone who steps out of line. People who advocate a different ideology and individual thought are hounded out through calls to (ironically) freedom of speech, or with accusations of 'unAustralian' and the general 'political correctness gone mad'.

Through all the noise the constant issue arises of what aspects of Australian life we are allowed to question and how we are supposed to do so. In Fair Day I have attempted to take on this challenge using the style of a contemporary and grotesque Italian genre, *cannibale*, to demonstrate the extremes that everyday Australian norms and attitudes can be taken to.

The national holiday of Australia Day provided a neat framework for a variety of aspects of Australian culture to be included in the story. Also, the day itself is seen as

sacrosanct by the dominant white culture, and attempts
to point out that the date itself marks the displacement of
Indigenous cultures more than any other event are fiercely
derided and resisted by those with a stake in that narrative
of national pride. While I think these critiques of Australia
Day are valid, they rightly come from those whom the
national pride narrative elides. As a white Anglo-Celtic
Australian man, my experience of Australia Day (and
Australia in general) will potentially be very different from
those of other backgrounds, but that is the experience that I
have and the perspective from which I can offer satire, and it
is hardly prudent for me to rewrite the cultural background
of others.

In the end it became a pleasurable experience to use the
cannibale genre to force aspects of my cultural background
into uncomfortable situations that required me to confront
aspects of myself I would have otherwise left unquestioned.
This process twisted and distorted the norms and ideals
I was taught at a young age until the reality of what I was
willing to accept in day-to-day life became a clear mess of
half-done ideas that have been cemented under the name of
'Australian'. The ideas around national pride and patriotic
significance caught up in the mythos of Australia Day were
simply begging to be warped in the delightfully deluded
cannibale way.

—ALEX DUNKIN, 2017

Also by Alex Dunkin:

COMING OUT CATHOLIC
HOMEBODY

Visit the author's website:
WWW.ALEXDUNKIN.COM

www.ingramcontent.com/pod-product-compliance
Lightning Source LLC
Chambersburg PA
CBHW021012120726
47905CB00009B/2968